MEDLEY OF FICTION

AN ANTHOLOGY OF SHORT STORIES
BY THE MEMBERS OF

Authors by Design

Edited by Terry W. Ervin and Carrie Chesney

Authors by Design
Medley of Fiction

AN ANTHOLOGY

Copyright 2008

ISBN: 978-0-9822029-0-6

Westmorland Publishing

First Paperback Edition: 2008

Westmorland Publishing

TABLE OF CONTENTS

Speaks Like Wind 11
    by Cynthia Bateman

Bloom Where You Stand 27
    by Sharon Kasenberg

To Preserve and Protect 29
    by C. L. Scarr

The Cross at the Edge of the Road................. 41
    by Lawrence D. Collins

Scrapbook of Memories 42
    by Virginia L. Fair

Prehistoric Verse 47
    by Cynthia Bateman

The Blue-Sprigged Dimity Dress 48
    by Tommie Lyn

Life Without You 57
    by Lawrence D. Collins

Green Like Her Eyes 58
    by Susie Hawes

Lady of the Well 61
    by Thomas E. Lynn

A Dark Sunset 68
    by Andrea Allison

The New Neighbour 69
    by Cynthia Bateman

Summer Portrait 71
    by Thomas E. Lynn

A Different Kind of Animal 72
    by E. J. Hayes

Nightmare 76
    by Randi-Lee Ryder

Jason's Disappearance 77
    by Jeannine Dufresne

Blood Diary 83
    by Andrea Allison

Natural Compensation 89
    by Mike Massey

Shades of Grey 110
    by Sharon Kasenberg

Acceptance 112
    by C. L. Scarr

Echoes 115
    by Dora Archer

For Lancelot 122
    by Carrie Chesney

Search and Rescue 123
    by Thomas E. Lynn

Finding the Calm 134
    by Cynthia Bateman

The Simplicity of It 135
    by Jia Lin

Eros at My Window 138
    by Robin Layne

Betrayal 139
    by Carrie Chesney

Mourning Song 150
    by Kechelle Barness

Author Biographies 151

SPEAKS LIKE WIND

Cynthia Bateman

Shadows grew long in the valley and a chill breeze rose up.
The first raindrops began to fall but still Speaks Like Wind knelt
by the grave, tears mingling with the rain on her face. Asleep on
the grass beside her lay her young son.

Suddenly, she arched her back, lifted her face to the sky and let
out a deep cry of pain. The child stirred at the sound and began to
whimper. Hearing his distress, she scooped him into her arms and
crooned softly, then stood and walked back to the settlement,
carrying her child. She was not yet an old woman. Grief had aged
her face beyond her years.

Speaks Like Wind lived with her husband's tribe in the cleft of
a cliff, high above the valley floor. In the side of a sheer rock wall,
it was reached by climbing a rope ladder. The cleft itself was large.
At the front of the cliff the opening was wide and high, going back
into the rock for several yards, fronting a series of connected caves
at the back of the cleft.

The hearth belonging to Speaks Like Wind was near the back
of the settlement. Smoke from other fires drifted back to her
sleeping area, filling it with the odors of cooking food and tobacco.
Her eyes often stung from the thick smoke. Clambering up the rope
ladder, carrying her child on her back, she headed there now.

"Talking to the dead, again, Speaks Like Wind?" taunted
Scowling Face as Speaks Like Wind walked by her fireplace. "It
won't do you any good. His spirit wanders the sky, looking for the
night wolf that killed him. He won't answer you. He can't even
hear you."

Speaks Like Wind hurried past ignoring Scowling Face, but
she could not ignore the old woman who now stood in her path.
Crab Cracker was one of the tribal elders, and she had purposely
stopped Speaks Like Wind.

"Child, the Council of Elders calls you this night as the sun
sets. Do not be late."

"Yes, Mother," whispered Speaks Like Wind as Crab Cracker turned away, not bothering to wait for a response. Everyone knew there was no disobeying a Council of Elders summons.

The rest of the afternoon passed slowly. Speaks Like Wind cleaned their sleeping area and laid out her best clothing to wear that night. Finally, it was time to go. She took her son to the neighboring hearth and walked toward the Tribal Council cave.

Nervous, she paused at the entrance to the council chamber. Taking a deep breath, she bent to enter the low opening. Seated around the fire in the center of the room were the men and women most highly revered by the tribe for their wisdom, courage and compassion, the Elders

Old Man looked at her gently. "Sit here, Daughter. Be warmed." He pointed to a place next to the fire.

"Thank you, Father," she replied. His kindness calmed her spirit.

Direct as always, Woman with Big Nose came right to the point. "It is time for your grieving to end," she said. "You have been without a man by your fire for many moons. Several of our men without wives have approached us and asked for your consideration. One in particular is quite interested."

Bear Hunter spoke in his deep bass voice, "The tribe can no longer afford to provide for you. To feed you and your child, we must take from another's pot. It has been a hard winter, and many pots are already empty."

Even as she sat by the fire's heat, her heart grew cold as she considered taking a husband.

"I know all the men of the tribe like brothers. Marrying one of them would seem...wrong."

"We understand that," nodded Old Man. "But there is one from the Osdack tribe who has shown interest in you and asked our permission to speak to you. He is your age, but has not yet taken a wife. He is waiting for you in the next chamber. Go in and talk to him, Child. Just talk to him."

"Yes, Father," she replied, her voice low with resignation. She backed out of the council room and turned toward the neighboring cave chamber.

•

12

Twilight was all that remained of the day as BearKiller of the Osdack tribe approached the cave entrance from a hidden opening at the side of the cleft. He was coming to meet a woman, or he hoped he would be meeting a woman. Her tribal elders had not promised she would come, only that they would ask her to meet with him.

Taking a deep breath, he stepped through the low opening into the darkness beyond and allowed his eyes to adjust to the dim light. The air was musty, bearing the scent of animals. He could see a low flickering, as if from a fire. Turning toward the light, he felt his way along the wall of the cave. Wiping his hand of the wall's dampness, he became aware of the sound of rushing water. As he continued on the air became fresher, and he knew he was near an underground stream.

The light grew brighter as he entered a high-ceilinged chamber. There was a small fire in the center of the room, and a stream ran along the edge. He realized how thirsty he was as he approached the water. He reached down and scooped a handful of the clear liquid. It was cold and sweet and perfectly quenched the thirst that had risen in his throat but did not quell the nervousness in his belly.

BearKiller was already waiting as Speaks Like Wind headed down the cave tunnel. The darkness inside the tunnel equaled the darkness in her heart. Her spirits continued to sink as she walked to the chamber. She did not want to speak to anyone about marrying. No one could fill the void left by her spirit mate's death.

Speaks Like Wind stood in the tunnel between the caves, her stomach clenching. She'd been holding her breath and was beginning to feel faint. She reached for the cave wall to steady herself, leaning down as she did so. Finally, she stood, straightening her back and shoulders. She wiped the tears from her face and, taking a deep breath, stepped into the room. She saw the figure of a man standing by a small fire. He turned slowly to face her.

Speaks Like Wind was silent as she approached the fire. She walked slowly, watching the man as she came. He stood waiting, also in silence. As she reached the center of the room they stood looking at each other from either side of the fire.

BearKiller saw a woman who had once been beautiful. Grief and pain had left their marks on her face. Now it held neither joy nor hope. She was small in stature with long sand-colored hair. Her eyes were large, golden brown and full of sorrow. BearKiller felt immense compassion for her.

On the other side of the fire, Speaks Like Wind appraised him. The flames lent a golden glow to his skin. He was tall and stood very straight. His face, framed in long black hair, was almost unreal in its perfection. His eyes were dark and wide apart. His nose was straight and his lips full and sensuous. As her gaze continued down she noticed well-formed, muscular arms beside a full chest and slender waist. Her eyes stopped when they reached his legs. His left leg was strong and clothed only in leggings, topped by his long tunic. His right leg, however, was heavily bandaged in leather strips. It was smaller than the left and misshapen. To stand straight he had to stand on tiptoe on his right foot.

"What happened to your leg?" she asked softly from behind the curtain of fire.

"When I was young a bear attacked my family. He grabbed my leg in his mouth and started to drag me away. I knew he would kill me if I did nothing, so I grabbed a stick and stabbed the bear's eyes. When he let go of me I continued to stab him until I killed him. That's how I got my name. I am BearKiller of the Osdack tribe. The bear caused damage to my leg that our shaman could not heal, and it has been like this most of my life."

"Can you hunt?"

"I have learned to hunt."

"Why have you never married?"

"Most women do not believe I can provide for them...and they do not find the sight of my leg to be a pleasant one."

Speaks Like Wind admired his honesty.

"Why did you come here?" she asked.

"I had heard that your tribe had a woman who had lost her mate several moons ago and had a child to care for. I hoped that such a one would be interested in someone like me."

Now it was his turn. "Why did *you* come?"

"I came because my elders asked me to."

"That is all?"

"That is all. My husband was taken from me by a wolf that stalked us in the night. Now they want me to remarry."

BearKiller could see the anguish on Speaks Like Wind's face as she told him this.

"When did this happen?" he asked gently.

"Eleven moons have passed since that time," she replied. "It was in the springtime. Now the elders want me to talk to you about marrying."

"What is your child's name?" asked BearKiller.

"I call him Creek because he loves to wade in the small river at the base of our cliff. He is only three winters and has already forgotten his father."

"I'm sorry to hear that. It is important for a boy to know his father. That is how he learns to be a man."

"Yes, well, I will have to do the best I can, I suppose."

BearKiller shifted his weight from his bad leg and stood tilted to one side. He continued to gaze at Speaks Like Wind through the fire and observe her expressions. Her face displayed every emotion she felt. Right now she was feeling awkward and uncomfortable. They had reached a deciding point - did they want to get to know each other, or would BearKiller just leave and never see her again? BearKiller knew what he wanted to do.

"I brought a gift for you"

"A gift?" she asked, with a lilt in her voice. "It has been a very long time since anyone has given me a gift. What did you bring me?"

He smiled. Her delight pleased him. He reached behind to his pack and pulled out a large package wrapped in aromatic leaves. He walked around to her side of the fire and handed it to her.

"Here. I hope you like it. I made it myself."

Speaks Like Wind took the package from him and held it up to her face.

"It smells wonderful. What is it?"

She began to unwrap the package. As she removed the leaves, her eyes widened and she held up a small sparkling-white fur robe, just large enough to cover her shoulders. The edges of the robe were black, and it was so soft that she couldn't stop touching it.

"This is beautiful," she whispered. "What is the fur?"

"Ermine." he answered, simply. "Here, let me put it on you."

He stepped back to examine the total look.

"You should always wear ermine. It suits you."

"But what can I give you in return?" she asked.

"I have not eaten yet this day. Could you give me an evening meal at your hearth?"

"I don't have much, but you are welcome to share what we do have."

"I would like that. Perhaps, before we go to your fire, I could snag us a rabbit or catch a fish or something."

"But it's dark. How can you hunt a rabbit or catch a fish in the dark?"

"Well, let me show you."

BearKiller made an extravagant bow and pointed her to the door of the cave. He scooped up two handfuls of water from the creek and threw them on the fire. Smoke billowed up, enveloping them as they walked through the cave entrance.

•

Outside, the sky was clear and the moon was just rising, casting its light across the land. Looking down from the cliff, BearKiller and Speaks Like Wind could see all the way across the valley. She spotted her husband's grave below and pointed to it.

"He lies there."

BearKiller looked down at the grave, then back at Speaks Like Wind's face. She was an injured soul. He understood her, or at least he felt that he did. He did not intend to hurry her away from her grief. He was surprised at the suddenness and strength of his feeling toward this woman he'd just met. He wanted to comfort and care for her. He wanted to protect her and her child from any more sorrow or pain. He did not want to leave her alone again.

She sensed his tension increase and looked up at him.

"What will you hunt in the moonlight?" she asked.

"A night creature. One who is also about in the darkness, like us. Follow me."

BearKiller turned and headed toward the plain that stretched away from the top of the cliff. Speaks Like Wind hurried behind him, stumbling over rocks and tufts of grass in the moonlight. Finally, he slowed and stooped behind a large boulder. Holding his finger to his lips, he pointed a short distance in front of them. There, stalking its own prey, was a small wildcat.

BearKiller reached behind to his pack and pulled out a small leather sling and several polished stones. Placing a stone in the sling's pouch, he stood. The only sound came as he whirled the sling over his head and let fly the stone. By the time the cat heard it, the stone was imbedded in the back of its head, and it had fallen to the ground, dying. BearKiller ran to the cat and picked it up by its tail. With a sharp rock, he slit its throat and held it high, allowing the blood to flow out freely. As the bleeding slowed, he carefully began to skin the cat. When he'd finished dressing the meat, BearKiller wrapped the carcass in the pelt and slung it over his shoulder.

"Can I help you carry something?" Speaks Like Wind asked him as he shifted his weight off his weak leg.

"No, I've got everything balanced. But we need to hurry. The smell of the cat's blood will attract larger predators and we don't want to be here when they come."

Speaks Like Wind looked over her shoulder fearfully and moved closer to BearKiller. The moon was high when they arrived at the settlement. The people of the tribe watched and whispered as they walked between the families. Speaks Like Wind could feel the fire rising in her cheeks at the stares of the other tribe members.

When they reached her hearth at the back of the overhang, BearKiller dumped the meat on the cooking hearth, and Speaks Like Wind walked to her neighbor, Raven's Eyes', fire to get her son.

From the back of the cleft, one stood watching her that Speaks Like Wind did not see. Tree Climber, one of the unmarried men of the tribe, watched her closely. He had seen her walk through the settlement with the stranger and was not pleased by it.

Raven's Eyes looked at her questioningly but she offered no explanation, only picked up her sleeping son and carried him back to their hearth.

BearKiller had already skewered the meat onto a spit and set it above the fire. As they sat near the fire, Speaks Like Wind and BearKiller talked softly. Their hunger heightened as the fragrance of the cooking meat wafted through the hearth. BearKiller sliced generous portions off the spit and they began to eat. By the time they'd finished, most of the campfires in the cleft had been banked for the night.

"BearKiller, why don't you stay here tonight? We have a sleeping area for guests."

He cleared his throat. "Yes, well, you're right. It is getting late and it's a long way to my home. I think I would like to stay here tonight, if you really don't mind. Can you show me where the sleeping area is?"

"I'll take you there, if you'd like. But do you have to go right now? Strangely, I find that I'm enjoying having you here!" She smiled mischievously, then laughed out loud.

"I would like very much to stay a little bit longer. I thought you might be getting tired, though. It's been an emotional day for you, hasn't it?

Speaks Like Wind was pensive as she looked out over the sleeping tribe. Somewhere on the other side of the cleft, a baby cried. They heard its mother's voice sing a soothing lullaby. The crying stopped and the cleft was quiet once more.

"Yes it has been an emotional day for me. It's been a day of discovery. I learned today that my tribe found me and my son to be burdens; that the elders of my tribe wanted me to remarry; that there was some man I'd never met who might want to marry me. And in the end, I discovered how much I'd buried when I buried my husband."

"What do you mean?"

"I mean that I'd buried laughter; I'd buried companionship; I'd buried adventure and new experiences. I'd buried feeling altogether."

Silence settled upon them as they sat by the fire, enjoying the presence of each other. Finally the fire began to die, and BearKiller stirred.

"Can you show me the sleeping area, now? I'm becoming very sleepy."

"Yes, I'll take you there. Let me check on Creek, first."

Speaks Like Wind leaned over her young son and adjusted his sleeping wrap, tugging it up under his chin. She tiptoed out and gestured to BearKiller to follow her. They crept around sleeping forms across the cleft.

"Here," she whispered. "There are sleeping wraps piled there in the corner."

"Do you rise early?" he asked.

"I rise when Creek does, and it's usually earlier than I would like! Don't worry about waking us. Come on over when you get up. I'll see you then." And she turned to head back to her hearth and Creek.

"Good night," BearKiller whispered loudly.

She looked over her shoulder at him. "Good night." She smiled to herself as she walked back to her hearth, unaware of Tree Climber's presence in the shadows of the cleft, watching her intently.

The settlement began to stir at daybreak. As sunlight stole up the cliffside, the households at the front of the cleft woke first. But BearKiller had been up before the dawn. By the time the Tribe was awake, he was returning from a hunting trip. As he clambered up the rope ladder and reached the top, he was greeted by several scowling men, the unmarried men of the Tribe. It was their responsibility to protect the settlement.

"Who are you and what do you want?" Tree Climber was the leader of the group, and it was he who now questioned BearKiller. He stood with his bow drawn, pointed at BearKiller.

"I am BearKiller of the Osdack Tribe. I am here for Speaks Like Wind."

"So, you are the one." The men stepped back and put down their weapons, whispering among themselves and stealing glances at BearKiller.

BearKiller carefully climbed up onto the cleft, never taking his eyes off Tree Climber.

"May I walk through?"

Grunting assent, the leader stepped aside and let BearKiller pass. One by one, the men stepped out of his way as he walked forward. Not looking back, he made his way through the settlement to Speaks Like Wind's hearth, carrying his kill over his shoulder.

Seeing him coming, Speaks Like Wind stood, waiting. She felt a small hand take hers and looked down to see her son also watching the tall man with the limp approach their fire.

"Maman, is that him?"

"Yes, Creek, that's him. What do you think of him?

"He's really tall...but he walks funny."

Speaks Like Wind smiled at her child's observation. Her smile grew broader as BearKiller arrived at her hearth. He stood before her and unceremoniously dropped four small fish and a brace of rabbits at her feet.

"I brought breakfast."

Speaks Like Wind broke out laughing.

"Creek, this is BearKiller. BearKiller, I'd like you to meet my son, Creek."

BearKiller leaned down to the child's eye level. He looked at Creek steadily for just a moment.

"Hello, Creek. Do you like fish?"

Creek slowly nodded his head up and down, indicating his assent.

"How about rabbit?"

Again, Creek nodded yes.

"Good. Can you help me skin these?"

Still, Creek only nodded yes.

"Here, you'll need this," and BearKiller handed Creek a small knife that fit perfectly in the child's hand.

"Where did you get that?" asked Speaks Like Wind.

"I made it. This morning. A man needs a knife, you know."

He turned to Creek. "Right?"

Awestruck, Creek still did not speak, but only nodded. He held the knife reverently in both hands.

"Well, then, let's go do it. Here, you take the fish." BearKiller handed the fish to Creek, then draped the rabbits over his own shoulder. He turned to walk away from Speaks Like Wind.

"Come, Creek. We have work to do." The man and boy headed over to the skinning area.

Speaks Like Wind watched them walk away.

"You must have thought well of him, hmmm?"

Speaks Like Wind was startled by Old Man's arrival.

"Yes, Father. I do. And it looks like Creek does, too."

"That's good. That's very good." Old Man mumbled to himself as he walked away.

Tree Climber watched the exchange between Speaks Like Wind and Old Man. His eyes narrowed, and he clenched his fists in anger. Tree Climber had spoken to the Elders about marrying Speaks Like Wind. He did not like being cast aside for a stranger.

BearKiller and Creek skinned the animals and Speaks Like Wind cooked the fish and rabbits, and the three of them ate heartily. She straightened their sleeping area, cleaned the cooking utensils and began to prepare the hides for tanning.

"Leave that until later, and let's take Creek for a walk." BearKiller stood smiling before her with his hand out to help her up.

"Maman, can we?" Creek jumped up and down excitedly.

Speaks Like Wind laughed and took BearKiller's hand. The three of them walked through the settlement to the rope ladder, BearKiller and Speaks Like Wind both painfully aware of the stares of the other Tribe members. Creek, however, was oblivious to them, tugging and pulling at his mother.

They reached the ladder, and BearKiller helped Speaks Like Wind and Creek climb down. As he put his foot on the first rung and turned toward the cleft to back down the ladder, he noticed Tree Climber standing off to the side, watching him intently. BearKiller lifted a hand and waved at Tree Climber, then descended the ladder.

Tree Climber did not return the wave. From the cliffside, he nursed his jealousy. Who did she think she was, rejecting him for a stranger from another tribe? This man was even damaged! Well, she wouldn't get away with it. He'd make sure of that. All through the day, Tree Climber thought of ways to seek his revenge. Finally, he devised a plan.

Wrapped up in thoughts of each other and enjoying their time together, Speaks Like Wind and BearKiller lost all track of time. It was only when Creek complained of hunger that they realized the day was almost gone and they were far from the cleft. BearKiller caught several fish for their dinner while Speaks Like Wind prepared a fire and lay a fur wrap on the ground for a place for the three of them to sleep that night. She was apprehensive about staying out in the open, thoughts of her husband, Lion Stalker, filling her mind.

Creek ate some dried meat they'd brought with them, and soon he was snoring softly, sound asleep. Speaks Like Wind picked him up and brought him to the fur, keeping him close to her. BearKiller brought the cleaned fish to Speaks Like Wind for cooking.

The flames leapt higher and higher setting the night ablaze as the fire took hold. Speaks Like Wind stared, mesmerized, at the quickening fire. BearKiller knew her thoughts were not of him, and he felt stirrings of jealousy in the pit of his stomach. Ashamed of such feelings, he busied himself turning the fish on the spit above the fire. The dripping juices made the flames hiss.

"Wind, what happened that night? Can you tell me about it?" His tone was gentle and caring, yet softly demanding. He wanted to know.

The question roused her from her reverie. She looked at him for a long moment, then returned to staring at the fire. Finally, without releasing her gaze, she spoke.

"We had been traveling all day. We were tired, very tired. Creek hadn't been walking long, so we'd had to carry him most of the way. We decided it would be all right if just this once we didn't make a fire."

She stopped and pounded her head with her fists.

"Oh, if we'd only made a fire!" came her anguished cry. "We didn't know a wolf had been following us most of the day. When we lay down on the ground to sleep, he attacked! He went after Lion Stalker, seizing his leg in his jaws. I grabbed Creek and ran. It was after daybreak when I arrived back at the settlement. I left Creek and took several of the men back with me. By the time we reached it, two days had passed."

Speaks Like Wind stopped speaking. She was finding it more and more difficult to breathe. Her voice barely above a whisper, she continued.

"The wolf had eaten most of Lion Stalker and what he didn't eat, other animals did. Only bones were left."

Tears streamed down her face as she recounted the grisly tale. Finally, she stopped, her body racked with sobs.

BearKiller sat silent, not moving. He could only imagine the horror of finding only the bloody bones of the person you loved.

Slowly, Speaks Like Wind's breathing calmed, and BearKiller moved closer to sit beside her. She did not seem to be aware of him at all. He reached up to put his arm around her shoulders and as his hand touched her arm she leaned into him. Burying her face in his chest she began to sob once more. This time he held her close and let her cry. Cradling her gently in his arms, he rocked her back and forth, speaking softly in words his grandmother had used to soothe him when his leg had first been injured.

They sat together into the night. Eventually, Speaks Like Wind fell asleep in his arms, exhausted. As her breathing slowed and deepened BearKiller laid her on the fur next to Creek. His arms were stiff from holding her, and his bad leg ached intensely. Adjusting the fur around her, he made sure she was bundled warmly against the night chill. He loaded the fire and lay down beside her.

He lay sleeplessly for a long time watching the stars overhead. Surprised at how quickly he had come to care for this woman and her child, he wondered if his feelings were genuine or borne of longing for a family of his own. What he knew for sure was that he wanted to protect them, both of them, from any more pain. His heart ached with want - want of a wife, a family, of *her*. And whether what he felt came from love or longing, he didn't care. He wanted to be the man at her hearth. Tomorrow, he would ask her.

Creek and the birds both awoke at daybreak. Speaks Like Wind tried to sleep just a little bit longer. BearKiller was having no trouble sleeping.

"Maman! Maman! Wake up!"

Speaks Like Wind slowly woke to a small face very close to hers, whispering loudly.

"Mama-a-n! Mama-a-a..."

"Yes, Creek, yes. I'm awake. I'm awake."

"Maman, I'm hungry!"

"Here. Eat this fish that we cooked last night. It will be good for breakfast."

Creek settled down to eating and became quiet for a few minutes. As he focused on his breakfast, the last lump under the fur began to stir.

"Maman, is BearKiller going to wake up?" Creek was back to whispering loudly.

"No, I'm not!" came a grumbly growl from under the fur.

With a squeal of delight, Creek launched himself at the fur bump.

"Creek!" Speaks Like Wind gave up to laughter as she watched Creek pummel BearKiller awake. Menacingly, the tall man rose above the little boy and attacked. Creek wiggled and giggled as BearKiller tickled him, rolling around on the fur.

"Stop, you two! We've got to get back to the settlement! Stop it!" Speaks Like Wind laughed as she spoke. Suddenly, a long arm reached out and pulled her into the fray. Squealing, she fell under Creek's tickling and wrestling, held fast in BearKiller's strong arms. Finally, their roughhousing slowed, and the laughter stopped. Reluctantly, Speaks Like Wind and BearKiller gathered their things, preparing to return to the settlement.

"Do we have to go back?" came Creek's plaintive whine.

"Yes, Creek, we do. There are things we must do. Come, now. Be a man." BearKiller spoke matter-of-factly as he hoisted the little boy onto his shoulders and began to walk back to the settlement.

Speaks Like Wind approached the cleft, following behind BearKiller and Creek and listening to BearKiller answer Creek's endless questions. This time she felt no embarrassment. She felt peaceful and happy, happier than she'd felt in months.

With the rope ladder in view, BearKiller decided to do his hunting before coming up, so Speaks Like Wind and Creek climbed up alone. Reaching the top of the ladder, Creek was clambering onto the cleft when an arm reached down and pulled him up. It was Tree Climber. With one arm around the boy and the other hand clamped tightly over the boy's mouth, he stood waiting for Speaks Like Wind to climb onto the cleft. Looking to see which direction Creek had gone, Speaks Like Wind reached the top of the ladder and noticed Tree Climber standing off to one side holding the boy. Creek's eyes were large with fright; Tree Climber held him so tightly, he couldn't move.

"What are you doing?" she demanded in a frightened whisper.

"I'm taking this child for my own. His father is dead. He needs someone to teach him our ways. You can't do it, so I'm claiming him!" Tree Climber spoke in a loud voice and acted strangely, as if he were drunk or had eaten some of the mushrooms that grew down by the creek.

By this time a crowd had gathered to watch events unfold. The tribe had formed a semi-circle around the trio with their backs to the rope ladder.

"Put my son down, right now! Put him down!" Speaks Like Wind was sobbing at the thought of losing her son.

"The only way I will put him down is for you to come with me."

"I would rather die!"

"Then perhaps your son should as well." Tree Climber had spoken quietly with an ominous coldness in his voice. He moved sideways a step to the edge of the cleft. Taking his hand from Creek's mouth, he grabbed him by each arm and held him over the edge. Creek screamed as he looked down to the valley floor.

"Stop! Stop it! I'll do whatever you want! Just put him down!"

"Son, what are you doing?" Old Man of the Elders spoke to Tree Climber in a stern voice.

"Why, I am simply taking a wife, Old Man."

Intent on the drama, no one noticed BearKiller climb up the rope ladder onto the cleft. Nor had they seen him move around the semi-circle of onlookers and position himself behind Tree Climber. Suddenly, an arm snaked out from behind Tree Climber to lock over his neck under his chin. At the same time another arm reached out and grabbed Creek by one arm.

As Tree Climber grabbed at the arm cutting off the air from his windpipe, he let go of Creek, allowing him to drop a little before BearKiller's grip on his arm stopped him. Holding Tree Climber firmly, BearKiller pulled Creek back up onto the cleft. He set him down and let go as Speaks Like Wind dashed forward to take her son from his grasp. As soon as BearKiller let go of Creek, he focused all his strength on Tree Climber. Tree Climber clawed more and more frantically at the arm around his neck as BearKiller steadily tightened his grip.

"My son! Stop!" Old Man's voice rose. BearKiller obeyed, loosening his grip without letting go. Tree Climber stood, still locked in BearKiller's hold, coughing and gasping. Several of the unmarried men rushed forward and took hold of Tree Climber.

"Take him to the Council Chamber immediately," Old Man bellowed. "BearKiller, you and Speaks Like Wind come, too."

Tree Climber's guards steered him toward the Council Chamber where the Elders were already gathering. Speaks Like Wind, still shaking and carrying Creek protectively in her arms, walked beside BearKiller to the Council Chamber. The rest of the Tribe followed close behind, crowding closely into the cave.

Old Man wasted no time. "Tree Climber, we all saw what you did. You cannot give any defense, for there is none. You threatened harm to an innocent child. You are banished from this Tribe for the rest of your days. Leave now."

The guards escorted him out of the cave chamber to the rope ladder. They stood lined up at the edge of the cleft and watched Tree Climber climb down and walk away from the cliff.

At the same time, in the Council Chamber, another drama was just starting.

"BearKiller, you rescued this child with no thought of the harm that could have befallen you. If you desire, you will be welcome at this settlement from now on."

BearKiller looked at Speaks Like Wind. Their eyes locked for a moment, and it seemed that a message passed between them.

"Thank you, Father. I would like to stay here, but only at one hearth." He looked at Speaks Like Wind and his eyes did not stray as he spoke. "I want only to make my home at the hearth belonging to Speaks Like Wind."

Old Man smiled and nodded. He looked at Speaks Like Wind. "Well, Child? What is your answer?"

Speaks Like Wind spoke, her voice barely above a whisper. "I would like that, Father. I would like for BearKiller to make his home at my hearth."

At this, their forgotten audience burst into cheers. Speaks Like Wind and Bearkiller had both known pain in their lives, and they knew they would have more. But for now, just for now, the pain was forgotten. They would have each other - and that was enough.

BLOOM WHERE YOU STAND

A young cactus in the desert
Surveyed the landscape drear,
And sniffing with disdain, she asked,
"Why was I planted here?"
I'm covered in horrid prickles –
A common shade of green –
Not that it really matters much,
Out here I won't be seen!"
She grew beneath the desert sun –
Became a lofty plant,
Tho' sun beat harshly down on her
And rain was very scant.
Her boredom was acutely felt,
Her life was full of woe –
She never understood that she
Was planted where she'd grow.
One day she happened to look down
And noticed something new –
In the coolness of her shadow
 A tiny cactus grew!
Its existence gave her purpose –
She felt parental pride,
An when it asked why it was there
In answer she replied:
"I didn't understand my worth
Until I saw you there –
You helped me see why I exist
And what I have to share.
I've come to see things differently
And comprehend at last
Just how much life is nurtured
 In the shadow that I cast.
Travelers rest within my shade
When their poor hides are baked –
They tap into the juice I yield
An find their thirst is slaked.
Birds nest within my shadow so

Their eggs don't end up poached!
You too will learn your usefulness" –
She heartily reproached.
Though my tale has been quite lengthy
It isn't finished yet –
In their season rains descended,
The arid soil grew wet.
Our cactus friend was soon adorned
In blossoms bright and bold
And stories of her loveliness
Both far and wide were told.
She perceived a different desert
When she was thus arrayed –
The beauty she embodied now
Was everywhere displayed.
We must strive to heed the lessons
The cactus came to learn
When we through trials and circumstance
For greener pastures yearn.
When life seems bleak and desert dry
Our purpose not defined,
We need to look beyond ourselves
To see how we're designed.
We each have capabilities,
Talents that we can share –
And if we try to nurture them
We'll bloom most anywhere!
Our confidence will be increased
And faithfulness expand
When we learn to trust the sower
We'll blossom where we stand.

By Sharon Kasenberg

To Preserve and Protect

C. L. Scarr

Arcanus, High Wizard of the Royal Court, nearly spit out his crumpet when the page tapped him on the shoulder and said, "Sorry to interrupt your breakfast, sir, but the king would like to see you." The lad placed a small envelope on the linen tablecloth, then darted away on his next errand.

The wizard frowned as he wiped his fingers and dabbed the corners of his mouth. The king hadn't asked to see him since that business with the telemarketers last spring. He picked up the envelope and removed the card it held. "Private study, 1:30 PM," he muttered and set the card down with a sigh. "Better get back to work."

He grimaced as he rubbed the throbbing joints in his hands and wrists, then hoisted himself out of his chair. As he left the dining hall, he mentally reviewed the small list of security breaches over the past few months. The Chasm of Indifference hadn't been bridged yet, but the enemies of Etheria were relentless. He tried to figure out what the summons could mean all the way back to his small apartment in the Security wing.

Keeping the dark forces from infiltrating Etheria grew harder every year, he mused, letting himself in. Over the past couple of years, he'd written a new set of incantations that he could use to mitigate the chaotic effects of a breach. He'd done his best to shield the country from the outside world, but he thought it wise to be prepared.

He sat down at his desk and picked up the sheet of parchment with the incantation he'd been working on for the past three days. It was designed to keep bond yield from plummeting in an upturning market. He had written others to control interest rates and unemployment and the cost of health insurance. He hoped the day would never come when he'd have to use these spells. But if the defenses he'd erected ever failed, they would help to maintain balance.

He spent the remaining time before his appointment trying to work, but he couldn't stop worrying about his upcoming audience with the king.

At last it was time to leave, and he ventured out of his spartan quarters into the bustling halls of the castle. Courtiers and other minor officials nodded as they passed him, but today he was too preoccupied to respond. When he arrived at the king's private study, he knocked, then waited for the call to enter.

The king sat behind an enormous mahogany desk, perusing a number of documents. He wore a charcoal gray three-piece suit with a red silk handkerchief in the breast pocket. Arcanus stood patiently waiting to be recognized. While he waited, he gazed at the papers spread before the king and quailed when he saw that they were brochures for spreadsheet programs and laptops and peripherals. The king had been shopping for computers again!

Just as he worked up the courage to point out the dangers of technology, the king looked up. "Arcanus," he said, "Thanks for coming by." Then a frown marred the stately features as he looked Arcanus up and down. "I thought we had a discussion about your wardrobe last time we spoke."

Arcanus looked down at his floor-length wizard robes. True, the fabric that had been so dark a blue that it looked black had faded and now showed wear spots. The once-bright gold stars and silver crescent moons now appeared lusterless and cracked.

"Forgive me, your highness. It seems I have been too busy to find a new set of robes."

"No, no, no. This whole robes-and-pointed-hat schtick has to go. It's the twenty-first century, for Pete's sake. You need to pick up some decent clothes. Try Marks & Spencer—or better yet, Abercrombie & Fitch."

Arcanus shrank inwardly as the words poured over him. "Er…Yes, your highness," he managed after a long pause.

"Anyway, about why I called you here. I've been looking at getting a few computers installed. They'd make—"

"Your highness, no! We've talked about this!"

The king raised his hand and said, "I know. Just hear me out. I'm aware that there are risks. But look at the benefits! It takes four people nearly a week to run payroll. With a couple of computers, two people could do the job in half the time."

"But—"

"Wait, I haven't finished yet. Look at your own situation. How long does it take to write one of your spells with that quill pen? With a word processor, you could do it in a fraction of the time. Do all your editing on the screen, then just click a button and print it out."

Arcanus felt as though his insides had been hollowed out. He bowed his head, desperately trying to think of some way to make the king see that once it started, there was no turning back. "With respect, your highness—"

"Save it, Wizard. I didn't think you'd agree, so I've decided to make some changes in personnel. I've hired an apprentice for you. Bright young man. Comes highly recommended. I want you to show him around, bring him up to speed."

The old wizard's mouth opened and closed, and he felt faint. "You want me to train my replacement? Your highness—"

Two loud knocks sounded on the chamber door in quick succession. Startled, Arcanus turned to see the door fly open. A young man breezed in carrying the scent of Aramis with him. Arcanus' first impression was of tanned skin, impossibly white teeth, and sleek dark hair. The young man didn't even glance his way but strode to the edge of the desk.

"Jason Selfridge, at your service." To the old wizard's astonishment, young Selfridge thrust his hand out to the king. Even worse, the king stood and shook the outstretched hand.

"Glad you could come aboard," the king said warmly. "I've heard great things about you."

"All true, I'm sure," the young man said and laughed without a trace of modesty. He snapped his fingers, and two business cards materialized. Selfridge handed one to the king and the other to Arcanus.

The king turned to Arcanus. "This is Jason. He's going to help you out, share the load. I want you to get him up to speed on your workload, the daily routine, that sort of thing. Stop in at the end of the day, and give me a progress report, will you?"

"Yes, your highness," Arcanus said. The words seemed to come out of their own accord. He didn't think himself capable of forming a more complex sentence. Fortunately, the king didn't seem to require him to say anything else.

"Good man. All right, then, I've got lots to do here." And with that, the king bent over his brochures again.

Arcanus left the room and wandered down the hall toward his quarters, his mind numb.

"Hey, old man," the new wizard called. "Where are you going? I thought you were going to show me around."

Arcanus pulled up short and turned to face his rival. For this man was, in fact, a rival. Here was no assistant or apprentice. This young pup was a wolf, hungry and eager for his first taste of blood.

"Very well. I assume you're familiar with the standard magical protocols."

"Of course. I just need to know how they fit in with the day-to-day court activities."

Arcanus gritted his teeth but proceeded to explain the system he'd worked out as they toured the castle. Then Arcanus showed Selfridge his workshop where a large map of Etheria took up most of one wall. Arcanus pointed out the defenses he'd put in place.

"This line here," he said, indicating the outer border of the kingdom, "is the Chasm of Indifference. It keeps the outside world from noticing us. Think of it as a virtual moat around the entire country, protecting our inhabitants from those who seek to possess or destroy their souls."

"Aren't you being a little melodramatic?" Selfridge asked.

"Not at all. Last year I visited another country where technology has run amok. Those people have been subjugated by microchips. They wear electronic devices on their persons, they work all day in front of computer screens, then they go home at night and stare at television screens or more computer screens. They're at the beck and call of the machines every single minute of the day."

"But the machines are useful. They provide entertainment. They make communication easier."

"Bah! They make it impossible to be left in peace. There is no surface that is not covered by advertising and no moment left unfilled by sound."

"Don't you think the people should be able to decide what they want?" Selfridge asked.

Arcanus peered at the younger man over his spectacles. "By the time they realize that there is a bad side to all the 'entertainment' and 'communication,' it's too late. Their children have been addicted to games and spend more time talking with strangers on the Internet than to other family members. The adults are unable to part with their mobile phones and pagers, and their bosses like it that way."

"I suppose," Selfridge said, his attention no longer on Arcanus.

Arcanus crossed the room to the supply cabinet where he stored the ingredients for basic potions and elixirs and opened the door. "This is where I keep—"

To the old wizard's annoyance, Selfridge shoved him aside and quickly ran a hand over each label. When he'd looked over the bottles and boxes on every shelf, Selfridge turned to Arcanus. "These are all standard grade. Where are the ingredients for technical grade potions and spells?"

Arcanus pulled himself up and stared down his nose at the impertinent youngster. "The king said that you're to be my apprentice. I hardly think you need access to advanced spells on your first day."

Selfridge said, "Wake up and smell the coffee, old man. I'm no apprentice. I graduated first in my class at age nineteen, and I've been working spells up to Level Five for over a year."

The young man was a prodigy—if his claims were true. A wizard wasn't supposed to cast spells that advanced until the age of thirty. Arcanus wanted to wipe the smug expression off Jason's face and replace it with the visage of some amphibious creature. "Really? Most impressive," he said. "In whose employ were these spells cast? Most governments have strict policies against underage wizards working above Level Three."

Selfridge's facial muscles retained the plastic smile he'd worn all day, but a malevolent glint came into his eyes. "Let's just say that my previous master was very progressive."

"Well, when I'm satisfied that you're competent to handle the advanced levels, I'll show you where the ingredients are stored," Arcanus said. "Until then, let's make do with these, shall we? Now if you'll excuse me, I have another meeting."

Arcanus turned on his heel and strode out of the room. His fists clenched and unclenched as he walked. He'd find out where this young shark had come from. He strode down the corridor, then ducked into an unoccupied sitting room. He pulled Jason's business card from the pocket of his robes and closed his eyes. He concentrated on forming a picture of Jason Selfridge in his mind, uttered the words of an informational spell, and touched the creamy surface of the card to his forehead.

A soft voice whispered inside his head, speaking as though it was reading from a resume. As the voice listed Selfridge's credits and shames, Arcanus grew more and more angry. Why, the little weasel hadn't graduated first in his class at all. He hadn't even graduated thirty-first in his class.

When the voice stopped, Arcanus opened his eyes. Of all the sneaky, underhanded, manipulative people he'd met in his life, Selfridge vaulted to the top of the list. He stormed out of the room, heading for the bureaucratic wing. He'd just have a word with the nitwits in HR. Hadn't anyone bothered to do a simple background check?

But when he arrived at their offices the door was locked. "Drat!" Arcanus said, and looked at his pocket watch. It was already past five, and he'd spent all afternoon with that schemer. He remembered belatedly that the louts in HR normally knocked off around teatime. Dejected, he walked back toward his quarters. On the way he considered his options. Simply exposing Selfridge's inaccurate resume wouldn't be enough; he had obviously provided the king with impeccable references, which would carry more weight. Arcanus knew he wouldn't be able to keep an eye on such an ambitious wizard, and he suspected that Selfridge would have his defenses in peak condition, even if Arcanus were inclined to try to do away with him. In the end, he could only think of one thing to do.

Back inside his apartment, he pulled a stepstool into his closet and snapped on the light. High on the top shelf, way in the back, an ancient leather-bound grimoire had lain untouched for the past thirty years or more. Grunting with the effort, he pulled the heavy tome off the shelf. Then he tottered over to his desk and set it down with a thud. He eased himself into his chair and adjusted his spectacles.

The grimoire held scores of the darkest spells ever conceived, collected by seventeen generations of wizards. He had hoped never to have to resort to using any of them. He wasn't even sure he'd find something useful now. Reverently, he lifted the book's thick cover and began turning the pages one by one. The calligraphy and watercolor illustrations glowed on the vellum pages. He'd forgotten how beautifully the spells were presented. They practically begged to be invoked.

He glanced briefly at a spell that would cause its target to become a deaf-mute. That might come in handy. There were other spells with more lethal consequences, and he passed them quickly. He shuddered when he came to the section that contained spells for bringing about exactly the kind of chaos that he'd been defending the kingdom against

34

for so long. And yet the illustration of one particular spell was too beautiful to pass by without admiring.

It was the spell for the Dark Rainbow, a supernatural bridge that could be built to cross the kinds of defense he had erected around the kingdom. There was no known counter-spell. Arcanus turned the page with a shudder.

He continued paging through the book. There were spells for creating plagues and darkness; there were spells for razing cities and killing livestock and poisoning municipal water supplies. He finally closed the book then stood up, stretching and yawning. He'd hoped to find an answer to the problem of what to do about Selfridge, but all he'd done was get depressed about all the bad things that magic could do in the hands of the wrong wizard. He shuffled off to his bedchamber and lay down. Maybe he would think of something in the morning.

Hours later, he awoke with a start. He threw the covers off and stumbled to the main room. He sensed something was wrong, and went to the window to look out. To his horror, the sky was purple. Huge gray-black clouds hung low to the ground, flickering with pent-up lightning.

He whirled and looked around the room, fearful that someone had stolen the grimoire. When he saw it still lying on his desk, he relaxed. Then he moved closer and noticed that the book was open to the page for the Dark Rainbow.

"Oh, no!" he said, "He wouldn't have!" He ran to the door and rushed into the corridor. Few people were awake yet, and he sprinted headlong to the end of the hallway where stairs led up to a tower. He took the steps two at a time, barely registering the pain in his knees. When he reached the room at the top, he yanked the door open and ran to the window overlooking the river far below—the river that marked Etheria's eastern border.

His heart sank as he beheld the scene taking place. Selfridge stood on the battlements of the outermost castle wall, arms up stretched. The Dark Rainbow was almost complete. The bridge itself was black—the absence of light. But the energy Selfridge pumped into it shot bolts of dark blue, purple, and maroon across its surface.

On the far side of the Chasm of Indifference, Arcanus saw the dark hordes gathering. He knew them to be snake oil salesmen, experts in the field of sales and marketing. They were telemarketers, spammers, and peddlers of electronic delights.

Arcanus groaned. Within hours, Etheria would be infested with X-Boxes, plasma TVs, crackberries, and Zunes. Within a week, a generation of young people would be turned into virtual zombies, and the older generation wouldn't be far behind.

He could no longer watch as the Dark Rainbow reached the other side. He stumbled away from the window and headed down the stairs. Blindly, he ran from the tower through the streets to find the wall where Selfridge stood, proud and triumphant. By now the first invaders were pouring across the Dark Rainbow. They jostled Arcanus as they passed, intent on reaching the untapped market Etheria's population represented.

"Why?" Arcanus shouted up to Selfridge. "Why did you do it? Who paid you? Was it Sony? Microsoft?"

"You don't get it, old man," Selfridge sneered. "I'm not on anybody's payroll. I just wanted to be the one to liberate the people of Etheria.

"Liberate? You've turned them into slaves as surely as if you had sold them!"

"Nonsense! I've made them happy! They'll thank me in the morning—they'll kiss my feet!"

Arcanus opened his mouth and closed it again. Such arrogance wouldn't respond to any logical argument he could make, and right now he was too upset for logic anyway. He turned his back on the young wizard, and headed toward the river. As he trudged along, he felt despair coming on. There was no known spell to destroy the Dark Rainbow once it was in place. What could he do? It looked like he was going to need all those incantations he'd written, after all.

"I can't let him win so easily," he said to himself as he neared the point where the Dark Rainbow was anchored on the Etheria side. The dark expanse emanated a sense of cold. It lacked the highlights and shadows of a natural structure, and the whole thing made his flesh crawl.

A few stragglers were still crossing, but it appeared that the main body of invaders had already flowed into Etheria. Arcanus took a deep breath and walked forward until he stood on the bridge. Immediately, all sound ceased. He was in total silence. He continued forward, and was unnerved not to be able to hear even his own breathing or footsteps.

When he reached the highest point of the arch he looked over the edge. He saw only the river flowing by on its way to the ocean. The Chasm of Indifference was, after all, a conceptual thing. It had boundaries, but they were invisible. The Dark Rainbow punctured that barrier. He continued on until he reached the other side.

The moment he stepped off the bridge, his ears were assaulted with a cacophony of blaring horns and traffic. He looked up and saw an enormous billboard whose message was reinforced by flashing colored lights. Above it, the sky was gradually clearing. The huge gray-black clouds had largely dissipated, but as he returned his gaze to the activity around him, he noticed that the air smelled of exhaust fumes and smoke.

He clambered down from the slight rise the bridge rested on, and walked through the crowded streets. Every shop window had signs and posters in it. Every light pole had advertising on it. He found the city square and stopped to stare when he saw a man and woman sitting side by side on a park bench, pecking furiously at their laptop keyboards. A trio of teenagers walked past him, each of them wearing earphones attached to a small device clipped to his belt. He wondered if these people had even noticed the strange clouds that covered the sky a short time ago.

Arcanus continued walking, observing the people and thinking about what he could do. What did they want? What was their weakness? He pondered the question as he watched them. Yes, he thought. There was something that he could do, but he would have to do it quickly.

He hurried back to Etheria, feeling an immense sense of relief when he once again walked its tranquil, picturesque streets. Now the lack of noise and clutter stood in stark contrast to the conditions across the border. He was grinning hugely as he strode back into the castle and made his way to the secret room where he stored the ingredients for technical grade spells. His grin disappeared the moment he arrived, though, and discovered that the seals and wards on the door had been broken. He rushed into the tiny room and moaned when he saw that all the cupboard doors gaped open, and many of the shelves were bare.

Arcanus cataloged what was left and determined what had been stolen. Whoever had broken in—and the only suspect was Selfridge—

had taken not only the ingredients for the Dark Rainbow, but also for several of the nastier spells described in the grimoire. Arcanus took the small satchel that was still on the bottom shelf of one cabinet and placed a few bottles and packets into it. He was grateful that the spell he planned to cast was so mundane that its ingredients hadn't interested Selfridge. When he had everything he needed, he left the room, not even bothering to conceal or protect it.

He raced back to his small apartment and grabbed a stack of parchment and his quill pen. He didn't have much time before this spell had to be cast, and it had to be right the first time. For the next hour, the only sound in his room was that of the pen nib scratching across the paper—or the sounds of paper being wadded up, and the ball hitting the floor. Scribbling furiously, he went through several drafts before he felt that he had something workable.

Satisfied at last, he set out, a fresh stack of parchment under his arm. His first destination was the main square. He tacked up a sheet of blank parchment in a prominent position, then cast his spell. The parchment bloomed with words and color pictures advertising the biggest electronics trade show ever presented—starting tomorrow in a town fifty miles away, far beyond Etheria's border.

Arcanus smiled as he stepped back, noting that the poster had already attracted the attention of two invaders. He continued walking through the city for the remainder of the day, posting sheets of parchment and filling them with the announcement. To the ordinary citizens of Etheria the poster would hold no interest. They hadn't had time to succumb to the lure of such things yet.

By the time he finished his rounds of the city, Arcanus was exhausted. But he still had one more task to complete. Wearily, he climbed the stone steps that gave access to the battlement where Selfridge had stood early this morning. He would have to stand watch here, waiting for his spell to bear fruit. Soon he saw the first of the invaders head back across the Dark Rainbow. Then, more of them set out of the city. Throughout the night a steady stream of the invaders answered the siren call of his advertisement.

Toward dawn, he was sure most of them had departed—at least temporarily. He wanted to wait for as many invaders as possible to leave before he cast the final spell in his arsenal, but he couldn't wait too long. The first wave of invaders could already be on their way back, if they'd figured out the trade show was a hoax. He was just about to say the words when he noticed a familiar figure heading toward the bridge. It was Selfridge!

He thought at first Selfridge had succumbed to the lure of his trade show poster, but then his shoulders slumped as he saw the king beside him. The two of them appeared to be deep in conversation. Selfridge gestured animatedly, seeming to point out the special features of the bridge.

Arcanus turned and ran down the stone steps leading to the street level. "Your highness!" he called. Pain wracked his old and tired body, but he forced himself on. He caught up with them just before they stepped onto the bridge. Selfridge looked startled and urged the king to keep moving.

"Wait, your highness, I beg of you," Arcanus said.

"What is it, Wizard?" the king asked.

Panting, Arcanus said, "I need to speak with you privately."

"Can't it wait?" the king asked. "Jason was just showing me this marvelous new bridge he built."

Arcanus had a sudden insight into how he could turn this situation to his favor. "It will only take a moment, your highness," Arcanus said. "But I don't want to interrupt your tour. I'll cross the bridge with you."

"Splendid!" the king said. He turned to Selfridge. "Lead the way, young man. Let's see this fine bridge of yours."

Selfridge inclined his head, then speared Arcanus with a glare before he stepped onto the bridge and started across. Arcanus and the king followed. From his first crossing, the wizard knew what to expect, but the king did not. Arcanus watched him closely as the sound ceased. The king looked startled, and glanced questioningly at Arcanus, who nodded.

They crossed quickly, and when they emerged on the other side, the king began speaking immediately. "Why did the sound stop? That wasn't at all what I was expecting." Then he looked around at all the bustle and traffic. "And what's this? Why is everyone in such a hurry?"

Selfridge stepped closer and said, "They're all very busy, your highness. They have important jobs, and they can react to any situation that comes up quickly."

The king frowned as he took in the garish lights and signs. At last he turned to Arcanus. "All right. What is it you wanted?"

"Your highness," Arcanus said, "The storeroom where I keep my most powerful potions was broken into last night."

The king frowned. "That's terrible. I'll have to get Security to look into it."

Arcanus looked at Selfridge, who suddenly seemed very interested in the giant billboard. He said, "My storeroom was protected by magic. The only person who could have broken in is someone else with wizard's training."

The king frowned. "Jason? Well, you *are* meant to be working together. He may be a bit eager, but look what he's accomplished."

"Yes, just look," Arcanus said. "Your highness, allow me to explain the purpose of this bridge." He laid out the facts quickly. "So you see, Selfridge here has opened us up to an invasion we're not prepared for. We have no defenses, no immunity. I predict that in a short time, our productivity will be severely decreased rather than increased."

When Arcanus finished, the king looked pale. "I had no idea!" he said. "Why would he do such a thing?" Without waiting for an answer, he turned to the young wizard and said, "Why would you do such a thing?"

Selfridge said, "You can't stop progress. In the long run you'll be better off. You'll be able to compete in the global marketplace."

The king stared at Selfridge for a long moment. Then he said, "You're fired. And if you ever try to set foot in Etheria again, I'll have you thrown in a dungeon so deep you'll think you're back in the Dark Ages. Are we clear?"

Selfridge scowled and said, "Crystal."

The king took one last disdainful look at the crowds of people rushing to work and said, "Come, Wizard. We don't belong here." He turned and headed back over the bridge.

"You know this isn't over, old man," Selfridge said.

"Maybe. But for now we still keep our way of life." He turned and crossed the Dark Rainbow for what he hoped was the last time.

By the time he and the king reached the castle, the sun had risen high enough to cast a rosy glow on the white turrets and gilded ornaments atop the gates. Arcanus was only able to enjoy the view for a moment, though. He realized that he needed to install a barrier on the Etheria side of the Dark Rainbow. He remembered a spell from the grimoire for an unquenchable fire. He didn't think the average telemarketer would be able to get through that. And he really ought to update his arsenal of counter-spells. He climbed the final steps to the main hall and sighed. A wizard's work was never done.

The Cross at the Edge of the Road

A monument to destruction. Memorial to waste
You see them on the highways all over the place
Telling the world of the sadness they bode
The little white cross at the edge of the road

The many lives that have suffered and died
Millions and millions of people have cried
The count is still rising, it's not even slowed
Another white cross at the edge of the road

How many times must the sirens be heard
Midnight calls discouraging words
Another innocent from which life flowed
Turned into a cross at the edge of the road

Lawrence D. Collins

SCRAPBOOK OF MEMORIES

Virginia Fair

COFFEE WITH PAPA

My parents had a routine of sitting outside in the back yard and drinking coffee in the evening when the weather permitted. I presume they started this ritual to find a quiet time for themselves away from us kids, or perhaps it started so they could keep a watchful eye on us. I remember one late summer evening as I eavesdropped on my parent's conversation I heard my father mention Viet Nam to my mother. He had recently returned from a tour of duty and never spoke of it. Having two older sisters and one older brother I gained my knowledge by listening to them talk about protesting the war and noticing the peace symbols and love beads that decorated their rooms. Too young to understand the depth of what my parents were saying, I tried my best to find a way to join in.

I was just seven years old, and I wanted to express how I felt about the war and how empty our lives were when he went to fight. I decided a cheer would be what my father needed to brighten him up, for as he talked with my mother I sensed sadness in him. With all the love I could muster, I started.

"Viet Nam! I hate Viet Nam! I hate the people in Viet Nam!"

To my confusion, my father grabbed me, swatted my behind, and sent me into the house. I barely recall my parents ever being physical with me in discipline. I fought back tears as I ran into the house, biting my lip, swallowing my shock. We never talked about the incident.

Sitting outside drinking coffee with my parents in my early teens, our conversation once again turned to the war. We discussed how the veterans were being treated badly in the United States, how it seemed the soldiers were being blamed for the war, and how the soldiers who came home felt about what had happened in Viet Nam. It was at that moment I began to understand why my father reacted as he did nine years earlier.

When I sang that cheer, I did not mean I hated the soldiers who were over there fighting for freedom, but those who initiated the war.

Conversing with my father that night I realized there would always be a fine line for the veterans on who they considered the "enemy" to be in Viet Nam. Thinking back, that one swat on my behind broadened my viewpoint. And I finally understood why he spanked me.

My father did not feel much like a hero.

FELINE APPARITIONS

When the leaves turn to rich hues of orange, red, and browns, and the weather cools, I know soon I will be inundated with ghost stories. Documentaries of the paranormal will be aired on television and fictional accounts of the spirit world written in magazines. I will avidly read and watch as many accounts into the realm of the surreal as my time will allow. My family has had many unexplained happenings in our life. I take comfort knowing others have experienced uncommon events, and that I am not alone.

Sensing things that are not there or events that might happen are traits common in my family. Every one of my relations has a story to tell of ghostly apparitions, premonitions, or dreams that appear real upon waking. I remember one particular dream my father had, a man normally well grounded to concepts of reality and not easily given into the frivolity of the unexplained.

For three consecutive nights he dreamt of a white kitten. It would lay sleeping at the foot of my parent's bed, then wake, stretch, and jump down onto the floor. He would steadily meet my father's gaze, mew softly, then disappear through the doorway that led into the bathroom.

My father always wakened at this particular moment, swearing he could hear kittens crying. Each time it happened, he went to the bathroom to get himself a drink. Before flicking on the light, he would see the feline apparition fade into the wall by the bathtub.

The last night after waking from this dream he reacted differently. Going to his closet, he pulled out his tools and sat down by the bathroom doorway. With hammer and chisel he chipped away, creating a hole.

The noise woke me, and to my disbelief I found my father purposely damaging the wall as my mother looked on in amazement. Both of us were certain his actions were the result of his nightly visitor. We didn't say a word, not wanting to make him feel foolish for his bizarre behavior.

When my father realized he was being watched, he lay down his tools and blushed, obviously embarrassed to be found in his boxers dismantling a wall because of a furry spirit.

"I must be nuts." He spoke softly as he began to clean up his mess.

"I'll make some coffee," mother remarked.

"Don't give up now, Dad. You've got to find out." I understood the moment had significance, and I knew if he stopped now his dream would continue to haunt him.

"You don't think I'm off my rocker?"

"Not in this family, Dad. What if your ghost kitty is in there? You've got to patch it up later anyway." I sat beside him and handed him his tools.

A few minutes later, he managed to make the gap large enough to see into a crawl space between the bathtub and the wall. He peered into the darkness, unable to see anything and mumbled something about me promising not to mention this to anyone. Disappointed, we sat in silence.

Mother returned, bringing coffee and a flashlight. My father shone the light into the empty space. Still he saw nothing. Once again, we resolved to never mention the incident. Mother noted there was still time before father had to start getting ready for work, so we sipped our coffee while contemplating our next move. Then, from the dark crevice between the tub and the wall, we heard a very soft sound.

I inched closer, positioning my ear to the hole. "I hear kittens!" I moved aside as my father shone the flashlight into the gap.

"They're at the other end." Quickly, he grabbed his tools and proceeded to chisel another hole by the front of the bathtub, working eagerly to get them. Soon, he was pulling out kittens and a distraught mother cat. The last one he retrieved from the cavity was the kitten from his dreams; the only white kitten in the litter. We concluded the mother cat had crawled into the opening from underneath the house for shelter and became trapped.

There are many possible explanations for what inspired my father to act upon his dream. He could have heard the muffled cries from the kittens, too low to register clearly but somehow placed in his subconscious. If this is the logical explanation, why did only the white kitten plague his dreams? What we do know is somehow my father received a call for help, and he answered.

JACOB'S PRISM

I sort through my photographs, looking at them one by one for those I would like to put in my scrapbook. There is the one of my father and his oldest brother carrying my cousin and me from the park, and there is one of my family on the couch celebrating Christmas in 1980. Though they evoke happy memories, neither fit together in a central theme. I spy the treasured box of pictures I took for my photography class ten years before. I hesitate for a moment, either to talk myself into looking at the photos or to talk myself out of it. I am not sure which. Slowly, I lift the lid. As my gaze falls upon the first photo I tremble.

The photo is black and white. My son and I stand in front of brick buildings in Old Sacramento, California. My pants and jacket are dark. From memory I know the color was purposely chosen for the illusion, black to illustrate the darkness that stirred inside of me. My neatly trimmed hair covers part of my eyes, as if I did not want to be seen nor see what lay before me. There is no smile on my face, and my eyes are closed, shutting out the world around me.

Where I stand the buildings across the street block the sunlight, leaving us in shadows. My son is behind me, dressed in a wind suit. The sun on that early spring day has warmed the air, and I remember just moments before the shutter clicked, he took off his jacket and tossed it aside. He stands turned away from me, his focus directed toward the sunshine at the end of the alley.

In the picture it appears as if my son is torn between two things: his desire to stay by my side, and a longing to explore the possibility of the world which waited beyond the alley. I remember I cried at the thought, distraught because he had been diagnosed with Attention Deficit Hyperactivity Disorder and now showed signs of Obsessive Compulsive Disorder. I feared for him, for I knew from researching and my own experience that depression would plague him throughout his life. Depression, a family curse handed down to my siblings, to my cousins and to me. A disorder which a beloved cousin had been unable to cope with and had eventually taken his own life.

I place the picture back in the box as my son comes running in from school.

"Mom, I have my report card." He tries his best to look sullen as if what he holds in his hands carries bad news.

"And?" I raise my eyebrow, trying not to give myself away and spoil the game he has grown so much to love.

"I don't think you will like it."
"Let me be the judge of that."

I hold the folded report card in my hands. I do not need to read it to know what it will say. I look at him cautiously as I hold the paper up, still folded in my hands. I glance sideways at him with my sternest look, as if his glum expression is telling me something I do not want to know.

"Do you need to tell me something before I read this?" I thump the paper against my palm waiting for his reply.

"I tried my best, Mom. I really did." By this time a giggle escapes him as he shuffles from foot to foot.

I play the game, but in reality don't hesitate to look for I know what it will read; grades in the high nineties. He is at top of his sixth grade class. At one time, due to his disorders, we felt he would fail academically. After all, he could barely talk nor could he read when he entered the second grade for the second time.

I hug him tight, cooing words of pride and encouragement to him. Persistence in getting him the help he needed early in life paid off. His teacher's comments state that he has a unique perspective of his world and because of this is an extremely capable student.

I know that I have not passed on a family curse, but instead a family legacy of creative uniqueness. His view of his surroundings is not limited due to his disorders but enhanced because of it. He sees the world not in black and white, but in Technicolor.

PREHISTORIC VERSE

A trochee fidgets
opposite an iamb,
while the dactyl hungrily
eyes the anapest.
The couplet feels inadequate
next to its heroic namesake
and the ballad is envious
of the ballade.
The light-hearted limerick skips
around the room,
carelessly bumping into
the epic,
who gazes down its
aristocratic nose in annoyance.
In the corner, the sonnet
stares doe-eyed at the lyric,
who nervously
looks away.
Thinking they are unseen,
the quatrain and the
sestet engage in a
tete-a-tete.
"Get a room" yells
the burlesque
and the haiku blushes wildly.

Cynthia Bateman

The Blue-Sprigged Dimity Dress

Tommie Lyn

Lisbeth Collins watched as her older sister sashayed past the young men who stood together talking after the church service. Ada Belle lifted her skirt slightly so the hem wouldn't drag through the red dust of the bare earth where the wagons were parked. Her hand drooped gracefully from her wrist, and she moved slowly, catching and holding the attention of the young men.

Lisbeth looked down at her own cream-colored dress with the faded remains of printed pink flowers scattered across the fabric, the worn line above the hem attesting to the latest lengthening of the skirt. She looked at Ada Belle again, jealous of the attention her sister garnered. At seventeen, Ada Belle was tall and beautiful, with a grace uncommon in one so young.

"You young'uns get in the wagon," Ma called. "Time we was on our way home."

All the members of the Collins family climbed onto the wagon unassisted. Except for three-year-old John. George swung him onto the back of the wagon. And Ada Belle, who had offers of help from two young men who seemed anxious to lend a hand.

•

"She don't need a new dress," Ada Belle said. "That one has lots of wear left in it."

"Ada Belle's right. You don't need a new dress," Ma said. "I'll hear no more about it. Now eat, and let your vittles stop your mouth."

Lisbeth knew better than to frown. She merely lowered her eyes to stare at her half-eaten supper of cornbread and warmed-over beans. She wasn't hungry now, but she also knew better than to leave uneaten food on her plate. She dutifully began eating, one bean at a time.

"Ma, look at her! She'll have me up until all hours washing dishes. She's just doing that because she's mad at me. Make her hurry up and get done," Ada Belle said.

"Lisbeth, don't dawdle. Finish your supper," Ma said.

Lisbeth cast a sideways glance at her older sister. Ada Belle always won. She knew how to get her way with Ma, and getting her way usually meant thwarting Lisbeth's desires, whatever they might be. Right now, her desire was for a new Sunday-go-to-meeting dress to replace the cream-colored hand-me-down Ada Belle had outgrown six years ago. Lisbeth had worn it for the last two years. She had been given the dress when it was too big for her, and now it had grown too small. But it had a lot of good wear in it yet. Ada Belle and Ma said so. A new dress was out of the question.

"I need you to go to the store. I'm just about out of flour. And it wouldn't hurt to get some coffee and sugar, too," Ma told Pa at breakfast the next day.

"All right. I need to speak to Llewellyn about something anyway," Pa said. "I'll start out soon as it gets light."

"Can I go, too?" Lisbeth and her younger sister Janie both asked at the same time. A trip to the general store was a pleasant diversion from their everyday routine, and Mr. Llewellyn sometimes gave each of the children a piece of hard candy when Pa bought a considerable amount of goods.

"Well, I guess you can go if you get your work done in time," Ma said.

The girls hurried through their morning chores so they wouldn't miss this trip to the store.

"Take Willie, too. And you look after him. And you mind your manners, now," Ma said as they dashed out the door when the mules pulled the wagon past the front of the house.

The mingled aromas of coffee, herbs, tobacco, leather and new fabric blended and imparted a singular ambiance to the store. Had Lisbeth been blindfolded and plunked down in Mr. Llewellyn's store, the richness of the combined scents would have told her where she was. She, Janie and Willie, exuberant at the prospect of going to the store, were silent and shy once they walked inside. They meandered slowly through the store, hands clasped behind their backs almost like a reminder not to touch anything.

While Mr. Llewellyn gathered the things on Ma's list, Lisbeth wandered through the different sections of the store looking at the ready-made men's shirts and collars, kegs of nails, and on to the table where fabric was stacked.

She spotted a new bolt of fabric. It was white dimity with sprigs of blue flowers, the same color as her eyes. She pictured herself wearing a dress made of it, her hair loosed from her pigtails, flowing free and cascading in shining waves down her back, a blue ribbon brought from under its mass and tied in a bow on top of her head. She saw herself mincing across the bare churchyard toward the wagon, holding her long skirt daintily, modestly, above the dusty ground, all eyes upon her, appreciation for her beauty inscribed on each face. She took a deep breath, and--

"Lisbeth!" her father said sharply.

Janie and Willie had already left the store and were climbing onto the wagon. With her eyes on the floor and a blush on her cheeks she hurried past her father and out the open door.

•

Sunday morning the Collins family rose, ate a breakfast of biscuits and gravy and dressed for church. Pa and George harnessed the mules, hitched them to the wagon and brought it to the front yard.

Sometimes they walked the two miles to the log church building, but today was the first Sunday of the month. The circuit preacher, Brother MacPherson, would be making his monthly visit, and there would be a dinner-on-the-grounds after the worship service. Ma had risen early, and with help from her daughters, cooked fried chicken, biscuits, bowls of vegetables, and her special cake with chocolate sugar icing. Pa and the boys loaded the bowls and platters of food onto the wagon behind the bench seat along with a box of plates and flatware, and Ma covered the food with a table cloth.

Ma climbed onto the driver's seat up front beside Pa while the girls took their places on the bench Pa had built for them behind the driver's seat. George, Willie and little John sat on the back of the wagon, their feet dangling from its flat bed like strings of dried peppers hung from the rafters in the kitchen. Pa clucked to the mules and started the wagon rolling toward the road.

When the wagon rattled to a stop in the churchyard, Ma and the children climbed down and waited by the door for Pa. He drove the wagon to the shady area where other folks were leaving their rigs and tied the mules to a hitching post. Pa joined the family, and they entered the cool, dimly-lit church building. They filed down the center aisle to their accustomed bench on the left side, two back from the front row, and sat.

Brother MacPherson sat alone on the front bench, as he always did. Lisbeth watched as he pulled his watch from his vest pocket and glanced at it. He raised his eyes, waited a few seconds, slipped the watch back into his pocket and stood. He walked to the pulpit and took his place behind it.

"Brothers and sisters, good morning. We'll start our worship today by singing 'Rock of Ages,'" he said.

He started the first stanza, singing almost an entire phrase before the congregation joined him. Lisbeth sang wholeheartedly, her voice slightly off-key at times. She loved going to church. She took pleasure in the singing, and she especially liked visiting with her best friend, Rhody Kilpatrick, after the service. The Sunday morning gathering provided an enjoyable social outlet for most people in this part of the north Georgia mountains.

When the singing ended and Brother MacPherson started speaking, Lisbeth rested against the back of the bench, settling in for another of his long sermons.

Her attention wandered from the preacher's thundering words as her gaze left his frowning face and dropped to her folded hands which lay in her lap. She noticed her dress had slipped up and exposed her knees.

That would not do. She grasped the hem and pulled the skirt into a more modest position, covering her knees. She released it, but when she put her hands into her lap again, it slipped back up. Lisbeth forgot her surroundings as she struggled with the unmanageable skirt. It defiantly reclaimed its position each time she released it, the pink crescents of her bare knees peeping from under the hem.

George poked her with his elbow. She looked up with a question in her eyes, and he discreetly pointed to Ma. Lisbeth raised her eyes to her mother's angry stare. She put her hands in her lap once more and leaned back. The skirt slipped up, exposing her knees. Ma's eyebrows arched, and she made a quick gesture with one hand indicating that Lisbeth should cover herself. At last, after an unsuccessful struggle to keep the faded fabric at an acceptable level, she pulled the hem of her skirt into position just over her knees and held it in place, a hand on each knee. She looked around at Ma, and Ma nodded. She sat leaned forward, hands on knees through the rest of the sermon.

After the last "amen" the congregation moved out to the shaded yard where the men set up makeshift tables under the trees. The women brought the dishes of food from the wagons and arranged them on the tables, chatting and catching up on news and gossip as they worked. They spread quilts on the ground near the tables where they could sit to eat their meal.

The children ran and played, enjoying the rare opportunity to be with friends and away from home, with its ready supply of chores. Lisbeth and Rhody Kilpatrick wandered at the edge of the piney woods alongside the churchyard, engrossed in girlish chatter.

Charlie Adair ran past them, chanting, "Lil Bit, Lil Bit," making Lisbeth's name into a taunt.

Lisbeth reddened, reached down and picked up a pine cone. She chunked it at Charlie, who ducked and laughed.

"Cain't hit me! Little Ol' Lil Bit cain't hit me! She's too little to hit a flea," he said and ran past her again, yanking one of her long black braids.

"C'mon, Lisbeth," Rhody said, glaring at Charlie's back as he disappeared behind the church building. "He don't matter. Don't pay no attention to him."

But Lisbeth stood looking down at her feet. "I am little. Even Janie's bigger than me now," she said.

"That don't matter--"

Rhody was interrupted by the call to dinner. After all the congregation had gathered around the tables and the children had been silenced by their parents, Brother MacPherson gave thanks for the food and the meal began.

The sun's rays slanted low through the pine boughs when people reluctantly began loading the remains of the feast onto the wagons for the homeward trek. All agreed it had been a fine day, and most hated to see it end.

Ada Belle had brought a small bundle from home. She retrieved it from under the bench seat and carried it to the Jackson's wagon. She would ride with them as far as the Widow McCready's house. It was her turn to spend a month with the elderly woman, who was unable to live alone. She had no children to care for her, so the young unmarried women of the congregation took turns staying in her home tending to her. Lisbeth watched as young men followed in Ada Belle's wake, each seeming to hope for the opportunity to hold her hand to assist her as she climbed into the Jackson's wagon.

Lisbeth sighed.

•

"I do need a new dress, Ma. This one is too short. And I'm already thirteen. Ada Belle got her first long dress when she was twelve."

Ma didn't answer right away. She looked at her daughter. "Well, I guess you're right about that."

"And there's not one of Ada Belle's old ones that I could wear now. You made the last good one over for Janie," she said.

Although Janie was two years younger than Lisbeth, her height surpassed Lisbeth's this spring. Now, Janie would be first to receive Ada Belle's hand-me-downs.

She took a deep breath. "I'll need a brand new one," she said.

"I don't know if we've got the money for that," her mother said.

"I could earn the money to buy the fabric. There's some dimity at the store. It has little blue flowers. . ."

Ma looked at the dreamy expression on Lisbeth's face and was transported to a time and a place she had all but forgotten, a time when she, too, had wanted a new dress, and her pa had bought the fabric for it. She cleared her throat and blinked the mist from her eyes.

"Ma, I have some money saved . . . almost forty cents. And I could collect more herbs. Mr. Llewellyn always wants more herbs. I can get the money to buy the fabric."

"You've worked months to get that forty cents. It'll be a long time before you have enough money just gathering herbs. And you need a new dress now," Ma said.

"But, Ma--"

"Maybe I could let you collect the eggs every other day and take them to the store and sell them--" Ma began.

"Really! You would let me do that?" Lisbeth said, a smile spreading on her face and her eyes glowing.

"I don't have no choice. You have to get the money so you can get that dress sewed. You're starting to look almost indecent in the one you have."

"Thank you, Ma," Lisbeth said.

In addition to doing her usual chores, she worked diligently collecting herbs, gathering eggs and taking them to the store every other day.

"Here you are, Lisbeth," Mr. Llewellyn said, as he counted out the money and laid it before her.

"Thank you," she said, picking up the coins and clutching them in her hand. She put the basket on her arm and wandered over to the table where the fabric was neatly stacked. She looked longingly at the pristine white dimity, its woven shiny stripes confining the exquisite sprigs of blue flowers in perfect alignment. She sighed and turned to go.

"Goodbye," Mr. Llewellyn called as she walked out the door.

"Goodbye," she answered.

After each long walk to the store to deliver eggs and herbs, she had more coins to add to the growing hoard she kept tied in the toe of a worn-out stocking. When she returned home, she took the stocking from the back of the dresser drawer, went to her bed, untied the knot and shook her riches onto the quilt. She added the new coins to the small pile and counted them all before she put them into the stocking and returned it to the hiding place.

It took almost three weeks to earn enough to buy the dress material. One evening after supper while she washed the dishes and Ma swept the kitchen floor, Lisbeth took a deep breath and said, "With what I'll get tomorrow for the eggs, I'll have enough to buy the dimity."

"Well," Ma said, "I reckon I'll have to go to the store with you tomorrow."

Lisbeth had a hard time falling asleep. She pictured herself wearing her new dress, seeming to float above the ground like a white petal floating on a smooth-flowing stream, elegant in her beautiful new gown. She imagined herself carefully spreading and arranging her skirt when she sat on the pew at church, and she saw herself graciously extending a hand to one of the young men who rushed up to help her climb onto the wagon. At last she drifted off, a faint smile on her lips.

She awoke at the first sounds of morning and dressed, then hurried into the kitchen to help Ma cook breakfast. The sooner everyone was fed and all the chores done, the sooner she and Ma could go to the store. And the sooner the dimity would be hers.

When they arrived at the store, she walked to the counter and set the egg basket on it. She wiped her sweaty palms on her dress and swallowed. After Mr. Llewellyn had counted out the money for the eggs, she took the stocking from the bottom of the basket and untied it. She shook the coins from it on to the counter with the others and pushed them toward Mr. Llewellyn.

She took a deep breath and said, "Mr. Llewellyn, I want to buy some dress material."

"All right," Mr. Llewellyn said. "Let me finish putting these eggs up, and I'll be right with you."

Lisbeth led the way to the fabric table, trembling with excitement. "Wait'll you see it, Ma," she said. "It's beautiful." But she stopped halfway to the table, tears welling up uncontrolled and spilling from her eyes like water pouring over the banks of a rain-swollen creek.

The dimity was gone.

Mr. Llewellyn walked past her to the shelves behind the fabric table. He leaned over to a low shelf and brought up the bolt of dimity. "This what you're looking for?"

She took a shuddering, trembling breath and said, "Yes, sir."

"I saw how you was always looking at it. Yesterday a lady come in and wanted it. I told her it was spoke for, and she got kind of huffy about it. So I thought I'd better put it out of sight."

Mr. Llewellyn measured out the yardage Ma asked for, cut it from the bolt, wrapped it in brown paper and tied it with a string. He counted out the amount needed for payment from Lisbeth's pile of coins and pushed the rest across the counter to her, adding a length of blue ribbon with the purchase of the blue-sprigged dimity.

Ma cut the pieces of the dress out of the fabric that afternoon, and Lisbeth began sewing her new dress. She sewed each morning after her chores were done, through the afternoon and late into the evening each day. Ma sewed the intricate seams of the bodice, while Lisbeth stitched the long seams of the skirt. She hemmed it and gathered the pleats into place at the waist, and Ma made over an old long petticoat to fit Lisbeth.

They finished the dress and petticoat on Friday.

On Sunday morning, the first of the new month, Lisbeth rose early, a flutter in her stomach at the thought of appearing at church in her dimity dress, the first brand new dress she'd ever owned. She bathed the night before, but she scrubbed her face again before slipping into her old dress to help Ma prepare the food for the dinner-on-the-grounds.

When it was almost time to go, she rushed to the room she shared with her sisters and put on her new dress. She unfastened her braids and brushed her gleaming black hair which fell in waves to her waist. Then she tied the blue ribbon in place, the bow on top of her head.

"Lisbeth! If you don't get out here this minute you'll have to walk!" Pa shouted.

When Pa pulled the wagon to a stop in front of the church building, Lisbeth carefully descended from the wagon and grasped her skirt with both hands, lifting it ever-so-slightly to keep the hem from dragging across the red earth of the church yard. She sashayed past the young men who were standing near the door, eyes straight ahead, seeming not to notice them.

"Who was that?" she heard Charlie say to one of the other fellows. "Not Lil Bit! Surely not Lil Bit!"

She stole a glance at him, at his open mouth. And a small smile curved her lips when she saw the shocked, then jealous look that passed over Ada Belle's face when she caught sight of her little sister entering the building.

Life Without You

Life without you I just can't comprehend
Our lives are connected, joined till the end
The life I consume is the life you expel
Life without you could only be hell

Life without you I would surely reject
No one to give love to or to respect
No dreams to live for, no one to call
Life without you would be no life at all

Life without you I would not understand
No one to talk to or walk hand in hand
No way to be happy, just boring and sad
Life without you would be crushingly bad

Life without you is a life full of woe
No one to visit, no place to go
A life full of anguish. days dark and blue
A life of depression is a life without you

Life without you would be dull and mundane
Day's full of sorrow, nights full of pain
A heart that is empty till my days are through
A life of torment is a life without you

By Lawrence D. Collins

Green, Like Her Eyes

Susie Hawes

They'll drink my daughter's blood. Her name is praised, her death honored. The priests treat us with respect, for my husband gave my Baby to them willingly.

Thunderous clouds obscure the moon. Tears blur my vision as I climb up the dirt path to the cold limestone rock beside the cistern. It's our only drinking water. The lake near my village is dead, poisoned with refuse. A grave for my Tia.

Four years I had my Baby girl, loved her and built my life around that child. Now she's alone in the lake where they threw her like so much trash. I've called out to her, praying, but I cannot hear Tia's sweet voice.

I open my mouth and rain falls on my tongue. The taste is unpleasant. Coppery, like blood; chilling, like my daughter's death. The bundle is light in my arms; its glow lights my way up the hill while my people sleep in the village below.

Her eyes were green; a miracle in our village of dark-eyed people. I thought I was blessed. Even in the midst of the famine I could always remember the color of our world before the crops began to die. All I had to do was look into Tia's emerald eyes.

"It's the drought," I whisper. "We're dying. The priests said that only the old gods could help us, and they required your life, Baby. Why should all of us die when only one had to?"

She doesn't answer. Before I lost her, Tia would sing to me, whisper secrets, share her heart with laughing emerald eyes, her tiny hand curled in my rough, work-worn fingers as though it were natural for a goddess to touch one such as I. So close, always so close to me, watching, singing, loving me. Tia hated to be alone.

The night is black, but a pale light glows from my bundle, illuminating a small circle around me as I kneel on the limestone rock. Dropping the bundle, I look at my hands now. Chaffed, red, empty.

Tears fall, mingling with the rain as it courses down my face. "It was your eyes, Baby. They were color of life, of green, growing things. The priests told us the old gods marked you for their sacrifice. I offered my body to them, but only you had eyes the color of life." I feel the sting as my nails dig into the palms of my hands. The pain comforts me.

My tired old blood wells up, and then mingles with the rain to stream over the lip of the cistern, falling into the darkness below.

"You would have died anyway, Baby. The cistern was running dry," I tell her, but the justification sounds weak. She was my child, my goddess, and I failed to protect her.

Her father was afraid of the gods. "It was him. He wouldn't let me take you away from here."

Only the pattering of the cold rain answers my plea.

The priests think they are right. Nature takes its course and the rain comes. Water flows down the shadowed cliffs above me, over the pale lip of rock where I sit. Rain water fresh and clean, filling our cistern with my Tia's blood.

The bundle slips from my lap, falling to rap against the limestone. The light around me is sharper now, coming from the untied bundle. I look down to see the little wooden doll that her father carved for her with his strong hands. The hands that gave her to the priests. Teeth clenched, I sweep it aside. It rolls, clattering across the pale rock and onto the mud. Light from my bundle shines on its wooden face.

Eyes painted green as poison, green as emeralds, faded eyes that stare at the blackened sky above like a corpse left to the gods to devour.

I watch as fat raindrops splash against those open eyes. What does Tia see, lying at the bottom of the lake? There are no fish to eat her eyes out, no weeds in that stagnant water to wrap around her. She's alone in the water, abandoned, entombed. Have the old gods come to comfort her? The gods that do not exist?

The memories come. Like a penance I relive every detail.

My husband cursed me. His rough hands gripped my arms as he held me back. Wind pushed against us as we stood on the beach. I struggled against him, forced to watch the priests carry her into the canoe. I smelled the water's stench and tasted its acid burn in the back of my throat. The soil was rough beneath my knees as he forced me down. I looked across the filthy waters and saw my Tia, bound hand and foot and held by the damned priests as they rowed to the center of the lake.

I saw the priests stand in the weather-beaten canoe. I relive it all, the surface of the lake as it brooded, the scum that coated it, my

Baby's wailing cry as they lifted her tiny, thrashing body above their heads. Her face was turned away so that I couldn't see her emerald eyes.

Such a cold and lonely death they gave my Baby. Hungry waters sucked Tia down like a delicious morsel, greedy, devouring her. I heard the voices of the priests as they called to their bloodthirsty gods.

Their gods, not mine. My goddess had emerald eyes.

Tia's thin cry stopped, just stopped, and I heard the splash of the water as her life was taken from me. Oily waves lapped at the beach, staining it with black sludge, feeding poison into the soil. My husband's hands released me and his footsteps faded. He left me to kneel beside my Tia's grave. Left me on the poisoned beach.

The soft pattering of rain surrounds me now. It fills my soul with hatred. I blaspheme gods that don't exist. I look down the hill into the darkness below and curse the people who killed her.

They'll come here to quench their thirst. The priests, my people, my husband, won't drink from the stagnant lake where Tia died. Here the water is fresh, given by their nonexistent gods.

I unwrap the rest of my bundle. Carefully I spread the plants out on the rock next to the cistern. The day Tia died I found them, poisonous weeds that grow in clusters at the water's edge. The plants glow, green like her eyes. Taking up the wooden doll, I smash them into a pulp. I free the lake's venom and watch as the luminous toxins mingle with rain water, bleeding death into the cistern.

My voice cuts through the pelting rain, but they will not hear me. "Who are you to live?" I shout at the village. Their doors are shut against the night. I sit in the darkness, waiting for the sun to rise.

Tia whispers to me now, after so many days of silence. She sings to her mother, rejoicing that she will not be alone. I give them to her willingly. When they begin to die, I will go to the lake and join my Baby, as well.

LADY OF THE WELL

Thomas E. Lynn

I found the well rusting and saw its abuse
From too little oiling and years of disuse.
As I peered down to gauge its depth, I could see
A sinuous reflection returning to me:
An indistinct image encircled so slight
In a halo that mirrored a soft glowing light.
I leaned somewhat closer with dubious eyes.
In deep concentration, I soon realized
That a ghostly sensation had risen in place.
On the water below . . . was a womanly face!

A cinnamon crispness embraced the New England air, a suggestion of autumn that wasn't rightfully due for a few more weeks. Paul Mason neared the end of a short hiatus from the rigors and grim relentlessness of another term at Stuyvesant College. Stuyvesant represented an elite learning center for affluent parents who preferred an impersonal boarding school environment for their offspring over the less than inspiring atmosphere of home. This was also the place where he instructed recalcitrant students in the illustrious history of their forefathers.

"Poor youthful wastrels," Professor Mason mumbled, "lost amid the rich and unwanted." He felt sorry for them because they knew so very little of their future place in society, and seemed not to care at all for their own genealogy.

His holiday was winding down but it would have been incomplete without revisiting the setting of his own youth, especially the now-abandoned grounds of the McHenry estate. He was so near now, just a few more miles. His pulse quickened with anticipation as his automobile slowed and finally came to a stop.

He observed the entrance gate standing open, and it was evident no visitor had been there for quite a while. He alighted from his car and stood for a moment. Perhaps a whisper of forgotten shadows enticed him to linger and to reflect upon the remnants and scant traces of yesterday.

Auras of the past caressed and flowed gently around him. His footsteps echoed dully on the shattered slate walkway as he retraced old familiar pathways. Paul visualized a two-story house with conical roof spires and tall shimmering white pillars on guard as silent sentinels. He experienced no desire to summon ghosts from dim recesses of his subconscious but, as he turned to leave, he noticed the well. Unkempt and secreted within the wild unbridled intertwining of braided vine and wayfaring ginger root, it was all that remained. Overgrown weeds and remnants of the foundation stood as sole sentinels of the past.

Once he tasted the cool bounty of this well and now felt drawn like a honeybee to sweet meadow clover. Brambles pricked his skin as he cleared away the undergrowth to clear the pump handle from wild entanglements. Leaning over to peer into the dark shaft, he suddenly experienced a ripple of dizziness and brushed the back of his hand across his face. It became necessary to close his eyes tightly until the wave of discomfort subsided. When he opened them again, he detected a faint reflection in the murky waters below.

It was surely imagination, but the longer he gazed into that deep chasm, the clearer the apparition materialized before him. "Strange," he thought, "how easily a person's mind can deceive itself."

The mysterious image swiftly assumed a more definite outline. The darkness within the well surrendered to an unearthly glow that emerged without explanation, and he easily identified the countenance of a woman's face. The image continued to manifest itself, triggering Paul's memory, and he recognized the reflection as the features of Amelia McHenry, someone he used to know, now dead these many years.

It was her father who founded the estate and, although several years older than himself, the two of them were close friends before her untimely death.

The spectral eyes of the watery visage burned hotly into his own and he was seized, unable to move. He felt their minds become attuned, and he was consumed with emotion of such magnitude that his heart momentarily paused in unrestrained alarm. A strange sensation overcame him, and along the fibrous passages of each frayed nerve of his body pulsed discordant impressions of hatred, betrayal, nd outrage. His very soul clamored for revenge.

But revenge for what?

The tentacles of memory undulated through him, searching for an answer. It was as if someone other than himself was in command, and after several moments he recalled the flames that blazed out of control forty years ago. The roaring of the fire and reluctant collapse of that great old house took him back to an earlier time.

It was the autumn of his twelfth year. A black wrought-iron fence, decorated with ornamental gladiators holding high their tridents to discourage curious boys from scaling its precipice, surrounded the McHenry estate. In spite of such a formidable obstacle, the groundskeeper was forever rescuing some hapless lad whose foot wedged tightly in the angled iron of that fence. Often, the ensnared victim was Paul himself.

Ambrose McHenry and his daughter were wealthy enough but not snobbish like their neighbors, the Kents, or even the Winthrops of equal notoriety. Mr. McHenry himself was a very tall man. Frequently stooping to talk to young Paul, he appeared to bend forward as if about to drop to his knees. In that position, Paul thought he resembled a human question mark. A long black beard emphasized the older man's appearance and character, but it was Miss Amelia whom Paul remembered the most. Although still a young woman, she habitually wore wire-rimmed spectacles perched on the end of her slender nose. Her black hair was knotted in a bun at the nape of her head in the manner of elderly matrons of that era. She spoke with a soft lyrical voice that rose at the end of each sentence as if encouraging some kind of response. Amelia was nearly her father's height. She also had his gaunt frame and asymmetrical face that rendered her somewhat less than attractive.

Paul, nevertheless, was captivated by her. In his young eyes, she was a real lady, and he sought her company at every opportunity.

He visited the McHenry estate with regularity — sometimes to run barefoot on the velvet lawn, but usually to walk with Miss Amelia through the rose garden. It was their private place where they discussed many things, their ambitions and their innermost thoughts.

"There is no one to help manage this huge house when my father dies," she once told him.

Paul felt surprised at her words. "Maybe I'll be grown by then and I can do everything for you." He exhibited the optimism of his tender age, and his response touched Amelia.

"I would like nothing better," she said, "but I fear my father may not be around for many more years. He is not well, you know."

Paul didn't know. He was sympathetic toward her and the possibility that she would some day be left alone. "Well, in that case," he spoke with a seriousness that belied his youthful age, "perhaps you should get married and have a husband to take care of you."

A wan smile played upon her lips at the suggestion.

"Jonathan Gorham is the only man who has expressed an interest in marriage," she whispered. "However, I'm afraid Mr. Gorham's attention is too easily influenced by the subject of father's money."

The insidious Jonathan Gorham was a visiting artist from New York. Engaged to paint her portrait, he was a guest of the house until such time as he fulfilled his contract. In the interim, he proved himself moody and petulant as well as ill humored and miserly. Not at all the type of suitor she would have preferred.

True to prediction, Ambrose McHenry passed away one night in his sleep. Paul grieved with his friend for her loss and regretted he was not yet of an age to help her as he desired. He consoled himself with the pride of being asked to sit alongside her in the family pew during the funeral service.

Summer neared the end of its reign, and the oaks and maples began to exchange their green leaves for the reds and yellows of fall. Paul and Amelia still walked in the garden and dropped pebbles into the old well, pretending they were magic tokens to make their wishes come true. Mr. Gorham's portrait of Amelia was now completed, and he would soon depart for his home back east.

"I shall be happy to see him go," she confided.

It was with great astonishment then that on the very next day, Paul learned of her elopement with the dour Jonathan Gorham. According to the McHenry housekeeper, she discovered a note pinned to her mistress' bed pillow advising of their hurried departure for Switzerland, and after a brief honeymoon would resume residence at the mansion.

Switzerland was half way around the world.

Paul was deeply concerned for his friend, especially knowing her earlier feelings for the strange fortune-seeking artist. What could possibly have changed her opinion about him so dramatically? Was Paul's concern generated because she was truly alone after her father's death? Questions plagued him about the suddenness of Miss Amelia's departure, but he would have to wait until her return to learn the answers.

He managed to fill the intervening days with school and evenings with his new job delivering newspapers. He developed a routine of riding past the McHenry estate every day on his bicycle, but there was no reason to pause or to stop there until Miss Amelia returned from her honeymoon.

Finally one afternoon, a black limousine drove through the front gate and stopped at the entrance of the McHenry house. It could only mean she had come home. Paul pedaled excitedly up the long driveway and ran across the porch to greet her. He rang the doorbell with their customary signal, two short rings and one long. However, rather than being welcomed by his friend, the door was opened by a sobbing housemaid.

What on earth could have happened? He stood for a moment, trying to interpret the maid's words through her uncontrolled weeping.

"Oh, young sir . . . our Miss Amelia is dead!"

Stunned at the news, Paul's joy quickly turned to sorrow and tears burned his eyes. "It can't be true," he stammered. "How can she be dead? She was on her honeymoon."

"Master Gorham just informed us," the maid continued through her sobs. "They were skiing, and she slipped and fell into an icy ravine. She died, and no one was able to recover her body. She lies buried there under the snow. We will never see her again." The sounds of loud mourning emanated from other servants within the house, and Mr. Gorham himself came to the door to confirm the news.

"I know you were her friend," he said gruffly, "but there is nothing you can do here. I suggest that you should go on home now."

Paul observed no sign of grief in the man's face or in his voice. His dislike for Mr. Gorham, manifested from the beginning sparked by Amelia's comments about him, immediately increased. It was his fault that Miss Amelia was forever gone and Paul knew the man married her only to get his hands on her money. He was certain that somehow Jonathan Gorham did away with her for that very reason.

There were other suspicions about the reported circumstances of Amelia McHenry's accidental death in a foreign country. Many concerned neighbors and friends attended the hearing to determine whether any unlawful acts were committed that would prevent the awarding of the McHenry assets to Jonathan Gorham as Amelia's widower and lawful heir. Nevertheless, no evidence of a derogatory nature was presented, and the New York artist was declared legal successor to the entire estate.

Paul would no longer be able to enjoy familiar walks through the garden and no more intimate conversations would be shared beside the old well. Miss Amelia was truly gone, and his visits to the McHenry estate ceased for all time.

Jonathan Gorham obtained the wealth he so fervently sought, but his victory was short lived. Only a week later, he perished in a mysterious fire that destroyed the mansion. Investigators reported that the blaze originated in the man's upstairs bedroom.

Paul heard the alarm bells and the sirens of the fire engines. He ran to the scene in time to see the white pillars collapse under the weight of a blazing roof. A crimson glow illuminated the night sky, and curious folks stood in twos and threes to watch the great house go up in flames.

"It's the worst fire I ever saw," a fireman commented. "And I was there when the cork factory burned down. A bad thing it was, too, but this is a hotter fire, and why that is I haven't a clue."

Now Paul Mason stood beside the old well and the memories returned in a flood. He was struck with the ambience of Miss Amelia's insomniac spirit. Staring into the water below, he was riveted in place and was treated to an eerie reenactment of her fateful adventure. Her ordeal at the hands of Jonathan Gorham unraveled before his eyes.

Transfixed, he witnessed more clearly through a dream, her dismissal of Mr. Gorham's services. Reluctant to leave, that gentleman renewed his request for consideration of marriage, behaving intolerably when he was once more rejected. He ranted and cursed, uttering vile threats until Amelia ordered him to leave her house immediately. Seeking refuge, she fled to her bedroom in fright.

He did so, but at an hour past midnight he furtively reentered the house, gaining entry into the chamber where she slept. Maddened with indignation and bent on exacting retribution, he struck her repeatedly with a heavy wooden candlestick holder. He then carried her down the staircase and unnoticed, tossed her body into the well.

Although her mortal remains lay entombed in a watery grave, Amelia's restive spirit was at liberty to move at will. Thus, she roamed the halls of the mansion in search of her slayer. Finally he returned and she immediately began haunting his every moment. She penetrated his dreams, tormenting him night after night, but he proved to be a strong adversary and thwarted her efforts time and again.

It was this obstinacy that eventually led her to create a spark from an electrical connection in the room where he lay in drunken slumber. She firmly secured the door and windows, watching as a flickering flame leaped to a lace curtain. Hungry fingers of fire swiftly reached out and enveloped the bed coverings. Gorham awoke and struggled futilely to open the door while flames and smoke engulfed the room. He hurled a chair at the window but the glass failed to shatter. Acrid fumes filled his lungs, and he slumped to the floor, gasping for breath.

Amelia's specter smugly watched as his body disappeared in the fiery rubble of the house.

Mr. Jonathan Gorham met his reward.

Paul remained unmoving while darkness enclosed him, and he sensed the full import of that horrible night so long ago. He soon realized that the image had vanished from the depths of the well and, although he deeply mourned for his friend, he was left with a feeling of serenity and satisfaction.

Remembering their many private talks beside the old well, Paul whispered a soft "farewell" to Miss Amelia. Turning, he walked away satisfied that his friend had achieved her revenge.

A Dark Sunset

Sitting on the mature blades of grass
Gazing at the great ball of fire descending
I realize something so bright and warm
Could also be sinister and frigid.

A peaceful symbol of compassion
Couldn't fill the gap
Hidden deep within my very soul,
But an overshadowing being makes the effort.

Sentimental thoughts and gestures,
An extended hand with love and kindness,
And a warm embrace helps fill the void
But only his kind heart lifted my emotional darkness.

I realize the pain that once was buried
Could be unearthed and destroyed
With not only the beauty of that sunset
But also with my love sitting beside me.

By Andrea Allison

The New Neighbor

Cynthia Bateman

Did you see their furniture? What did you think of it?" whispered
Marcy in a conspiratorial tone. Not bothering to wait for a response,
she continued. "It was ghastly! All those animal prints everywhere! It
looked like it came from a brothel!"

Georgia just looked at her. Marcy was the neighborhood gossip.
You didn't say anything to her if you didn't want the whole block to
hear a "juiced-up" version of it.

Right now, she was staring out Georgia's front window at the
moving van across the street. The new owners of the house directly
across from Georgia's were moving in, and Marcy was watching every
step.

Georgia busied herself picking up newspapers and coffee cups
from breakfast. "Marcy, would you like a cup of coffee? I've got some
freshly made. Come on in the kitchen with me, and I'll pour you a
cup."

"Mm. No thanks"

Georgia heard her gasp and hurried into the living room. "What is
it, Marcy?"

"There she is! There's the owner! Oh my gosh! Look at her!"

Georgia glanced out the window to see a woman wearing a short
skirt with an elaborate hairdo and a great deal of make-up walking
across the street toward Georgia's house.

"Oh no! Here she comes! Get rid of her, Georgia!"

Georgia looked askance at Marcy as she answered the ringing
doorbell.

"Hello. You must be my new neighbor! Welcome to the block.
Can I help you with something?"

The woman smiled brightly at Georgia's greeting. By this time, a
scowling Marcy had walked to the door and stood sternly directly
behind Georgia.

"Uh, yeah, hi. I'm Cassandra. Thanks." Cassandra looked warily at
Marcy. "Um, I was wondering if you could do me a huge favor?"

"Sure, anything."

Looking back at Georgia, Cassandra's face relaxed into a relieved
expression. "I've got to go to a performance over at the Village

Theater. This is my first time as an actor with the group. But, as you can see, the movers aren't finished yet. Could you do me the tremendous favor of watching the movers and making sure nothing gets dented or broken or…whatever?"

"Of course! I'd be happy to. What part are you playing?"

"I play the prostitute in Of Human Bondage. Can't you tell?" Spreading her arms wide, Cassandra threw back her head and laughed. "I really don't usually dress like this! In fact, I'm usually very conservative. I have to be. I'm the counselor for the Women's and Children's Free Clinic down on Third St."

"How interesting." Georgia turned and looked over her shoulder at Marcy. "Cassandra, this is Marcy, our neighbor from down the street. She was just admiring your furniture. Right, Marcy?" Georgia continued without giving Marcy a chance to speak. "I would be more than happy to stand guard over your furniture. You go on and have a great performance. When you get back, you'll have to tell me all about it so Marcy and I can go watch you. Right, Marcy? And I'd love to hear about your work. That must be really fulfilling. Right, Marcy?"

"Oh, it is. Especially when I work with children. You may have noticed all the animal print furniture the movers unloaded. That's for my den, where I counsel children of abuse. They just love the soft texture and all the wild prints."

"Oh, really? Isn't that interesting, Marcy?"

"Well, I've got to dash. Thank you so much, Georgia. Nice to meet you, Marcy." Cassandra walked back across the street and climbed into a cute little sports car. A teen-aged girl was already in the passenger seat, waiting.

"Come on, Mom, we've gotta go. We're going to be late!"

"I'm coming, I'm coming. I just met a couple of our new neighbors. Georgia is a gem, I can tell. I'm not sure about Marcy. She didn't say a word. She must be the quiet one in the neighborhood."

Cassandra gunned the engine, and the sports car roared away.

Summer Portrait

I like a drowsy summer
and a lazy wistful day
When skeeters hum their little tunes
and bullfrogs croak away,
Where fireflies greet the twilight
with luminescent glow
And I can sit 'til heart's content,
a-rockin' to and fro.

It makes me feel all tingly
like a child at Christmas time,
Like a hound dog chasing rabbits
or a poet penning rhyme,
And when I gently close my eyes
in unexpected slumber
The stars and angels gather round
in undetermined number.

A man could live a long, long time
in such an awesome place
With nature for a neighbor
and memories to embrace.
Oh, if I could paint a masterpiece
for all the world to see
I'd paint a drowsy summer day
for lazy folk like me.

Thomas Lynn

A Different Kind of Animal

E.J. Hayes

Every girl has her time of the month. For this one, it's a little different.

I thrash and twitch on her creased sheets, and she gives in to me without a murmur. It's cool outside, but I'm hot, because the moonlight burns on her naked skin.

Each moon it's a different room, a different city, but always it can see me, the fat, grinning thing with its stolen light, and its gravity is indefatigable. I'm like an asteroid, trapped in eternal ellipse, hurtling at last towards glorious reunion after drifting in the freezing dark from the other side of forever.

Since the last full moon, anyway. Somehow, it seems pointless.

Defiant, I try to lie still, but the conquest is beyond my control. Like a heartless lover, I invade her. I open her eyes — my eyes, now — and the ceiling lurches towards me; the walls shudder and threaten. Her hair bristles, and my mouth waters until she drools. It's time to go.

Outside, the night tastes cosmic, of time beyond prediction or memory. I can taste the summer that's coming, last week's rain, the unsavoured future, the unending backstretch of history. Indoors, there's no such perspective. It's drowned out by the hopeless, transient reek of human death.

Most of the time, she can't smell it. Most of the time, she's just a girl. Her life is a dreary montage of dusty trains, pawnshops, the smoky bedrooms of men who use her, city after city, all too finite — but with a purpose. They all have a purpose, even if it's just to die.

My purpose, as I stretch her limbs to fit mine, is not apparent.

Each time the greedy moon fattens, I awaken, and I crawl inside her where no one can see. Every month, for a few days, she's mine to use, until she dies and I must find another — but what for? Every month, I hurl my questions at the moon, and I get no reply. Only this mute, useless compulsion to kill.

Already, I'm at the door of the club. The moon has dragged me up, dressed me, walked me out into the street. Good old moon, taking care of things while I'm busy elsewhere, listening to my bones harden and tasting the slow thickening of my blood.

The place is dirty, dark and packed with humanity. The primordial frequency of the music vibrates in my stinging ears. I smell countless startling details, a hundred desperate lives. They smell good. I like this place. The girl chose it, subconsciously, when the moon was silent. She doesn't know me yet, this latest one, but she's done me well tonight.

I stand at the bar. The darkness is gritty on my hands. I get a drink, and I chug, and I get another. By the time the second splash of spirits slides down my throat, I've chosen one. He's over there, behind me, though I haven't yet looked. Not old, not young, not special. He smells of dirt and death and his brief, wasted life that has already begun to end. They all smell that way. It's something I got used to a long time ago.

But I crush my senses in closer, and there's more — the starry white metallic taste of some dirty tab he's dropped — and I lick my lips, disappointed. When it's contaminated, it's like digesting rat poison. Last time it happened, I was sick all over the floor. With a diet like mine, a projectile spew isn't pretty.

I swallow, bitterness stinging my mouth, and search on.

In a moment, here's another, a sharp point in this blunt mass of imminent death, and this time I turn, and I open my eyes. He's a long way off but I can see his dull, ferrous irises. His lashes are gummed at the corners, and I can feel him looking at me. No, really. I can feel his gaze. The ambient fluorescence reflecting off my body to his retinae is thrumming and tangible. The fact of his perception creates a surface tension, in my moonlit sight, of which he's unaware.

Most of them are unaware, of so many things.

I pluck his thoughts from the smoky air, and I taste them. The banalities of human contact that are so vital. They persist after a hundred thousand years: who is she? Does she see me? Has she got anything that I want?

At this time of the month, they've all got what I want.

Bristles rise along my spine, and I swallow the rest of the cheap moonshine without tasting it, savouring instead the heat inside me when it hits my stomach and boils. I stalk him, hidden by the crowd until I'm ready. My fingertips sting me as I reach for his arm.

He doesn't see me. None of them see me, not even when the moon's full. What they see is the girl: torn stockings, dirty black hair, dark lipstick in a pale face. Tonight, she's not herself. Tonight, she's me — an elusively flawed clone, a subtly different kind of animal — and they never see me until their time's nearly gone.

He doesn't say a lot, this one. Good. I'm not much interested in talking. His hands are hot, and his mouth tastes of bile and bourbon and the cheap green in his homemade cigarettes. Forgetting where we are, I crush his lip between my teeth. What the...? Swallow. Sorry. Take me outside. Okay.

An alley, smelling of dark and grease and garbage. I push him down and climb onto his lap. He takes hold of me and even though he's drunk to hell, his effort is honest enough, until I bend my head and bare my growing moon-time teeth and slowly crush his throat.

I swallow, and tear, and swallow.

As he dies, his body takes over, and gives genetic eternity one last shot, so to speak. Only later, I wonder if he felt it.

Lucky for this girl that there's nothing it can do to her now. Like I said, I'm a different kind of animal.

Chew. Swallow.

I'm gorged, and my back arches, and I lift my head to that insatiable moon — but I snap my teeth closed just in time. In the twenty-first century, howling is so passé. If the moon is displeased, it gives no sign.

Stand. Stretch. Shake.

I take the money — she'll need it, when this is over — and the gold. The rings fit nicely on my fingers. As I admire them, the physical distension of my stomach informs me that I'm no longer hungry, and my brain agrees. Yet I know I'll go back in there, and choose another one, and another.

Rise. Be. Eat. Live forever. Kill, until that smirking moon is satisfied. That's it. That's all there is.

I exult, like they do, in the pointlessness of it all.

Sniff.

Someone's there, behind me. Someone followed me outside. In my imagination, his essence is already running down my throat.

Sniff again.

I open my mouth and breathe, savouring the aimless taste of my future. And then I smell it. It's on him, all over him, in his hair, on his breath, in the vodka-scented sweat that's yet to break out on his skin.

It's the smell of this, this endless life of mine. The smell of the first hot-blooded beast that ever bested its prey, and of every unlucky animal that ever died screaming in its struggle towards the top of the towering food chain. It's the smell I rise for, live for, kill for. The smell I've hunted for, unknowing, since the moon first birthed me. The smell of me.

I slaver, and blood washes off my chin.

Somewhere in our basest evolutionary programming — somewhere so large, perhaps, that it's invisible — all animals are the same. Eat, breathe, sleep. Mate.

Like my prey, whose last, desperate act was wholly genetic, procreation must be my reason for being. If not to perpetuate, what purpose have I?

My soul vibrates to the triumphant moon, and I turn, and see him at last.

He smiles at me, this other one — such a human thing to do — and with my yellow moon-time eyes, I can see the jagged outlines of his teeth. I can taste untold years of him on the scintillating air. I can hear the immortal lifeblood in his wolfish heart.

I stretch my jaw, lolling my tongue across my teeth. Hungry, canine teeth that I see now were only ever a means to an end. Together, he and I can give that lazy moon what it wants at last.

The girl's children will harbour our children. When her babies are old enough, my children will lift their heads to the sky and see their destiny, gleaming fat and white with the useless light of unheeding stars.

Maybe, after a while, the moon will have no further use for us. If we procreate as animals do, then surely that thing most animal — that final, most human end — is not beyond us?

Yet, I'm infinitely, cosmically satisfied at last. He's everything I've ever wanted in a man, and I've waited countless years to meet him. To die for me — to die with me — is, I think, the very least he can do.

Nightmare

Reaching out, fingers curled
gnarled branches of flesh
gripping
frantic cold
Pulling, snatching
  down
    down
caressing
velvety soft kisses
brush my cheek.

Gossamer wings fluttering
powerful arms lift
   up
  up
holding tight.

Eyes open wide
searching wildly
cold sweat,
deep sigh
eyes close sleep descends
dream.

Randi-Lee Ryder

Jason's Disappearance

Jeannine Dufresne

I sat in my son's room and stared at his picture for the longest time. Today was no different than yesterday or any other day since Jason's disappearance. The rain gently tapping on the window brought back memories of the day Jason wanted to run away when he was six years old. He'd packed his duffel bag with food he had taken from the kitchen cabinet along with dog food for his Golden Retriever, Sparky. I remember laughing so hard when Jason opened the door and noticed the heavy rainstorm. He turned to me and said with his cute innocent face, "I'll wait till tomorrow."

I picked up his pajamas, brought them to my face and cried as I smelled his scent on the cotton fabric. I felt so sorry for Sparky who sat by the front door day after day, waiting for his companion's return. I'll never forget the events of that dreadful night.

It was a Monday evening in late June. The weather was cooperating and, although it was humid, there was a cool breeze which felt refreshing. My husband and I were sitting in the park next to the other parents, waiting for our son's baseball game to begin. Since their uniforms weren't ready yet, Jason wore his favorite Spiderman T-shirt, and a black pair of pants.

As I diverted my eyes towards the crowd, I noticed a young toddler on a tricycle next to a bench where an old man sat, filling his pipe with fresh tobacco. The old man called after his grandson.

"Eric, don't go too far. Stay close to Grandpa. I'm just going to rest for a few minutes, then you can ride your bike."

I returned my gaze towards the field just as the game was starting.

"Come on, Jason!" my husband and I cheered as our son picked up his bat.

Jason was tall for his age. At twelve years old, he appeared older than the rest of his teammates. While stronger on the outside, he tended to be overly sensitive on the inside

I noticed my son was distracted. Instead of watching the pitch, his eyes kept wondering towards the crowd. I sensed he was nervous because he wanted so much for his team to win. Jason was very competitive, a quality he inherited from his father. When he finally returned his attention to the pitch, he swung a little too early, pulling the ball foul and into the row of spectators.

Poor little Eric had no idea what was coming when the ball slammed into the side of his head. The blow knocked the little boy and the tricycle to the ground. The child lay unconscious on the grass.

I could feel panic from parents and spectators filling the air. My heart went out to the old man who kneeled down next to his grandson and cried out for help. My head spun and my heart raced as I rushed towards the little boy. Every movement seemed like it was on fast forward when I looked around me. I saw someone reaching for a cell phone to call an ambulance. The boy lay unconscious while people hovered over him, trying to help.

Suddenly, my son's teammates started pointing their fingers at Jason and shouting, "He killed him!" My boy started crying and, as if in a daze, he wandered off. My husband, Jeffrey, and I called out, "Jason, come back, son!" But our boy never turned back. I saw him dashing across the street.

As I started running after him, I heard my husband's footsteps right behind me. I tripped on a rock and fell flat on my stomach. When my husband stopped to help me up, I shouted, "I'm okay, go find Jason!"

By the time the paramedics arrived, Eric was conscious but not out of the woods. After the ambulance rushed him to the hospital, some of the parents offered to help search for Jason. As the ambulance's siren faded, Jeffrey returned, but without Jason. I just about lost it. I yelled at the top of my lungs for Jason, but my son was nowhere in sight.

Jeffrey and I, along with a several other parents roamed the neighborhood all night but never found him. I felt so drained and empty when I walked into the house. I called his friends but nobody had seen him or heard from him since he left the park.

An hour later, Jeffrey and I walked into the police station to file a missing person report. I felt restless as my husband and I sat in the chair opposite from an officer with dark eyes and wire-rimmed glasses and watched him write information about our son on a pad with curled-up edges. I checked my cell phone every minute in case Jason was desperately trying to reach me.

Once we left the police station, Jeffrey and I headed home in the hopes that Jason would be there waiting for us. But there was no Jason. I immediately reached for the yellow pages and started searching for a private investigator. I looked at a few names, and I finally decided on one. I wrote down the information on a piece of paper, and I called the investigator's office to make an appointment. Luckily, he had a spot available that same afternoon.

When I entered his office, I was greeted by a man who was skin and bones with a head full of hair and a boyish look. He invited me to sit in a brown leather chair while he walked to the other side of his desk and sat down. I started explaining the reason for my visit when I was interrupted by the sound of his phone.

While he answered the call, I looked around his office and noticed it was almost empty except for his desk and a filing cabinet. It looked as though he had just moved in for there were unopened boxes stacked near his filing cabinet. In the corner, near the window that offered a beautiful view of the lake, a plant desperately needed attention.

After I explained my case and asked him about his credentials and experience in similar cases, I felt reassured and immediately hired him to find Jason. I gave him a picture of my son, paid his retainer and left, hoping I was a step further in finding my son.

On the third morning of Jason's disappearance, I sat at the kitchen table working on my third cup of coffee. All I'd lived on for three days was coffee and cigarettes. After quitting three years ago, I picked up the bad habit shortly after Jason's vanishing and was quickly up to three packs a day. Jason's Golden Retriever sat at my feet. The poor dog followed me everywhere as if he was afraid I would disappear too. It's amazing how close I became with that dog. I even found myself taking him for walks, trying to fill the void inside of me.

The sound of the doorbell interrupted my thoughts. With Sparky at my side, I opened the door and found myself face-to-face with the private investigator I'd hired. He handed me a manila envelope and said he had found a little boy matching my son's description. With my trembling fingers, I removed a glossy print of a boy on a railroad track. There was no mistake that it was my son. Although they were covered in dirt, I recognized the Spiderman T-shirt and pants he was wearing the last time I saw him. I caressed the picture with my fingers and started crying.

I reached for the phone and nervously dialed my husband's cell. My fingers were shaking so much that I had to redial twice before I finally got his number right. After I calmed down, I read the investigator's report to my husband. It appeared that Jason had last been seen at the railway station in Toronto.

After I hung up the phone, I headed towards the kitchen to get a cup of coffee when I realized I had forgotten all about the private investigator. He stood patiently by the door, waiting for further instructions. I thanked him for his quick response in locating my son and told him I would contact him if I needed anything else. After he left, I immediately called the police to inform them of Jason's whereabouts.

My husband pulled into the driveway less than thirty minutes after I announced the good news. He had booked tickets for us on the next flight to Toronto. After my mother picked up Sparky, I immediately packed a few things in an overnight bag, and we headed to the airport. Once the plane took off, I couldn't sit still. I glanced at my watch and noticed that we'd only been flying for fifteen minutes. When the plane finally taxied up to the gate at Pearson International Airport, I undid my belt and grabbed my bag in the overhead cabinet. My pulse was racing as I rushed towards the exit. My husband placed his hand on my shoulders and mouthed words of encouragement. We headed towards the taxi stand and jumped into the first available cab.

"Union Station please!" I heard my husband say to the driver. I looked out the window and carefully scanned all the sidewalks for signs of Jason. The drive to the train station seemed to take forever as the taxi moved slowly through the heavy traffic.

After we searched the terminal for about an hour, an eerie feeling came over me. I felt like my legs were going to give out on me. I couldn't help imagining the worst. I carefully scanned the faces of the homeless people sleeping on the floor. I didn't want to give up searching for my boy but, frankly, I was beginning to feel like we might be too late. Maybe Jason decided to get on another train and was on his way to another destination by now. Feeling exhausted and desperate to see my son, I collapsed on a bench and started crying. My husband sat next to me, placed my head on his shoulders and rocked me like a baby. Suddenly, I heard him say, "Carolyn, there he is!"

I lifted my head and directed my watery eyes to where my husband was pointing. All I saw were two lovers embracing near the coffee shop.

"Where do you see him?" I asked my husband, almost pleadingly.

"Over there, by the water fountain," he said, grabbing my hand. "C'mon!"

My husband and I ran toward the fountain, and the moment I saw my son I screamed with joy. I rushed to his side and hugged him tightly. I looked into his face, and what I saw frightened me. Jason looked so scared and lost. "My poor boy, how could you run away from us like that?" I asked. "You must be hungry! Are you hurt?"

My son looked at me, and the first words that came out of his mouth were, "Eric…is he…Did I kill…?"

I put my arms around him and said, "Eric's fine! He had a bad headache for a while but he's okay!"

"How did you get here, son?" Jeffrey asked.

Jason looked at his dad and explained his journey. "When I left the park, I took a bus to the train station and sneaked into a cargo wagon. A few hours later, I found myself at Union Station. I met this homeless guy, Paul. He showed me how to survive." My son then took us to meet Paul. It was hard to see his face beneath all the dirt. He was a small man with long salt and pepper hair. The trench coat he wore was a few sizes too big and it swept the sidewalk with his every move.

My husband took money from his wallet. My eyes were getting watery and I couldn't tell how much he had taken out, but I saw my husband folding the bills and placing them in Paul's hand and saying, "Thank you."

"Thank you!" I exclaimed, feeling grateful for the person who had looked after my son.

Paul glanced at the bills in his hand and stared at my husband with the expression of someone who had just won the lottery. He let out a hollow cough before saying, "Thank you."

Jason looked up at me and said, "Can we get a hamburger?"

I answered, "Of course."

Jason grabbed my hand and said, "Mom, can Paul come with us? He loves hamburgers, don't you Paul?"

Paul nodded.

"Paul, would you like to join us?" my husband asked the man who had been a part of my son's life for the past three days.

I noticed a smile on Paul's face as he nodded and said, "Thanks."

I kissed the top of my son's head and looked at my teary-eyed husband. The three of us hugged and held on to each other as we walked out of the terminal. When we reached the sidewalk, I let go of them, removed a pack of cigarettes from my purse and threw it in the trashcan. "I won't need them anymore," I said, hugging my husband and son tightly.

As I held on to my family, I saw Paul reach into the garbage and retrieve my pack of cigarettes. He placed it in his pocket and followed us down the street.

"Mom, did Sparky miss me?" Jason asked as we made our way through the crowded sidewalk.

"He sure did! I know a dog that's going to be very happy tonight!

BLOOD DIARY

Andrea Allison

Leyla searched for months to find the perfect office to start writing her new novel. Her apartment was too small and uninspiring. Moreover, she hated to be cooped up all day. She stood before a grotesque building, staring at her new professional haven. The rest of the block was new. Most of the other buildings had been restored to their former glory days, but this one was never touched. Interesting enough, no one seemed to mind either. It was as if they accepted it as the odd one out, which made it that much more appealing to her.

"Hellooo? Leyla?" Raina said. "Wake up, girl. According to you, we have a lot of work to do."

"Sorry, it's just so mesmerizing. Don't you think?"

"What planet are you from?" Raina said. "Here on Earth this is a Hilton for the homeless. The other buildings are laughing at it."

"So, it's not fancy. But it's cheap and close to my apartment. Besides, you haven't even seen the room yet. It has lots of potential."

"If you say so." Raina rolled her eyes.

They approached the front door guarded by two eroded granite sculptures. As they walked through the lobby, Leyla examined the room which played host to scattered trash, peeling wallpaper, and broken furniture. It looked like a tornado swept through, and no one bothered to clean up.

"This place is really growing on me," Raina said.

"Will you please stop with the sarcastic comments?"

Raina put up her hands in surrender.

"Thank you. The stairs are this way."

"Stairs? You didn't say anything about stairs. What's wrong with the elevator?"

"Well...it's kind of broken. It's only a few stairs. You'll barely break a sweat," Leyla said, biting her lower lip. Raina reluctantly nodded and followed her to the stairway.

As they climbed, Raina complained, "Oh, sure. It's only a few stairs. I feel like I'm climbing a tower. You couldn't tell me about this yesterday?"

"I know, and I'm sorry. But look at it this way. It's exercise," Leyla said, panting heavily. "We only have one more flight to go."

They struggled up the last few stairs like toys winding down. After taking a short breather, they proceeded down the narrow, graffiti-covered hall. "Here we are." As Leyla slid the key into the lock, she continued, "Raina, prepare to be amazed." She tried to turn it but the key wouldn't move. Leyla jiggled the knob until it finally gave. The door squeaked as it swung opened.

"Oh! What is that funky smell?" Raina said, masking her nose and mouth. "Did an animal die in here or what?"

"Ummm...no. The smell is new." Leyla dashed to the window. She pulled and pulled, pleading for it to open. The window finally released its grip. "Maybe if it airs out for a little while, the smell won't be so bad. Other than that, what do you think?"

Torn floral wallpaper exposed the dull lime color paint. Unidentifiable stains tainted the hardwood floor. The only object occupying the room was an old radiator nestled in a corner.

"Well...," she shrugged and continued, "I guess it has potential. But do you really want to put money in to transforming this place?"

"I understand what you're saying, but I still want to do this. It's not going to cost all that much. The electricity is already connected, and there is a decent restroom down the hall. All I have to do is take down the wallpaper and add a few coats of paint. Strip the floor and polish it. Have a phone and DSL line installed. I have all the furniture I need in storage. It is going to be great when it's finished. I just know it."

For the next week, Leyla and Raina worked inexhaustibly making the room presentable. After Leyla finished painting the window trim, she laid the brush across an open paint can while watching Raina reveal the refinished floor.

"What do you want me to do with these sheets?" Raina asked.

"Just put them in a pile somewhere. Since we're almost finished, how about I go and get us something to eat."

"I'll go. The paint fumes are starting to get to me."

"All right. Could you put these extra brushes in the car, please?" Leyla asked, handing the brushes to her. "Wait. I have one more." She walked over to the paint cans near the window. "That's odd."

"What's wrong?" Raina joined her. "What? It's just a can of paint."

"Yes, but I just laid a paint brush on it a second ago. Now it's gone."

"Are you sure? Maybe you already gave it to me."

"No. I set it right here," she said, pointing to the can. "Things have gone missing all week. First, the trash bags, then an entire can of paint, and now a paint brush. What's next?"

"Don't worry about it. I think someone has been stealing our stuff," Raina said.

"I don't know." Leyla sat down, arms crossed against her chest. She took a few deep breaths.

"Calm down, girl. It's no big deal."

"I know. But I think it's a sign. I feel that maybe my dream is turning into a disaster. Yeah, the supply disappearances are pretty trivial. But what if this is just the beginning of something worse?"

"I don't think I've ever seen you like this. What happened to that happy, confident girl last week?"

"I don't know. It seems like the more time I spend in this room, the more depressed I feel," Leyla said, wiping a tear from her cheek.

"How about we get out of here for a little while. Let's go get a few slices of pizza at Joe's. We'll finish this later."

Leyla knew going out would do her some good, but an overwhelming feeling convinced her not to. "You go. I'll stay here and maybe clean up a bit or unload a few boxes from the car."

"Are you sure?"

Leyla nodded.

"Ok. I'll be back. Don't have too much fun without me," Raina said, winking.

Leyla didn't acknowledge her friend's reluctant exit. Instead, she began packing up supplies. As she packed, Leyla noticed a small box hidden under a metal folding chair. "Where did this come from?" A black light sat nestled inside the mysterious box. *It couldn't hurt to see if this room had any secrets.* She turned off the lights and pulled down the shade. Positioning herself in the middle of the room, she flipped the switch.

"Don't tell me it needs batteries," she said, shaking it vigorously until it finally worked.

She examined every aspect of the room. Leyla couldn't believe what she found.

An hour passed before Raina returned. Leyla waited patiently on the floor with the black light clenched against her chest.

After switching the light on, Raina asked, "What are you doing sitting in the dark? Better yet, why are you on the floor and what is in your hand?"

"Turn off the light," she mumbled, gazing at the wall.

"Why? What's going on?"

"Turn the light off now."

Raina hesitantly flipped the switch. Once the room was dark, Leyla turned the black light on again.

"Oh my god. What is that?"

"I'm not sure," Leyla muttered, "but I think it's blood."

"Are you sure it's blood and not paint or something? What language is that?" Raina asked, admiring the hidden words.

"I read somewhere that the only way to see blood undetectable by the naked eye is with a black light. I think it's someone's diary."

"What language is it? Do you know what it says?"

"Yeah, it's Spanish." Leyla stood and shone the light on a particular section. *La angustia es tortura en el alma de una persona. Usted sufiria apenas como tengo.*

"And that means what?"

Leyla ran her finger under each word as she translated. "Basically it means: Heartbreak is torture on a person's soul. You will suffer just as I have."

"Oh please. This is just some stupid prank. Didn't this building used to be a college dorm at one time?"

"Yeah, in the 80s I think. I don't think this is the product of a bored teenager, Raina. I can't explain it, but something is really off about all this."

"Whatever," Raina said, stumbling her way to the light. "I think the paint fumes are starting to get to you, Leyla. Let's call it a day. We can go to RJ's, have a few drinks and flirt with some guys. It'll be fun."

"What? No. I'm not leaving. Not after finding this," Leyla said, sitting on the floor.

"Are you crazy? I'm not leaving you here." Raina struggled to pull Leyla to her feet, but she wouldn't budge.

"I'm not going anywhere," Leyla said, folding her arms like an angry child. "If you want to leave, just leave then. I'll be fine." A voice in the back of her mind told her to go with Raina, but she couldn't shake the urge to stay.

Raina pleaded for her friend to come with her but Leyla stood firm with her decision.

"Fine. Stay then. It won't be my fault if something bad happens to you. I don't know why I even try anymore," Raina said.

Leyla watched her friend storm out of the room. She felt like a ferocious dog ready to attack. But once Raina was gone, Leyla's anger disappeared. *What just happened?* It felt like someone took complete control of her thoughts. Leyla dashed to the door, desperately trying to open it. The knob wouldn't budge.

"Not again. Come on. Open." As she tugged on it, Leyla noticed a shadow creeping up the door, slowly swallowing it. Her heart pounded like a drum. Her breath accelerated. Leyla backed away. The room's temperature dropped with every step she took.

Suddenly, the air became very heavy, making it a bit difficult to breath. Something brushed against her shoulder. Leyla spun around. Nothing was there. A cool breeze swept passed her. She made another full circle. The dark figure broke away from the door. It crept slowly toward her, changing form. Leyla tried to scream but nothing came out.

She fell against the wall and slid down. Curling into a ball, she prayed for it to go away. Tears flowed down her cheeks. After a few minutes, Leyla pried her swollen eyes open. It was gone.

Leyla had no clue what happened and didn't care. She bolted to the door. "Please open!" Turning the knob, the door opened with ease. She sprinted down the hallway. Just as Leyla was about to enter the staircase, Raina climbed the remaining steps.

"Whoa. What's wrong? Did someone attack you? I knew this was a bad idea."

Before Leyla could speak, her mind started to spin. Her vision became obscured. Her legs buckled as she collapsed to the floor.

Leyla woke to bright lights and a killer headache. After adjusting her eyes, she began to analyze her surroundings. "Where am I?" she mumbled.

"You're in the hospital, sweetie," Raina said, holding her hand. "You passed out. How are you feeling?"

"Pretty much everything aches."

"The doctor said you may have been exposed to some kind of gas leak. He said you should be fine in a day or two."

"Gas leak? Are you sure?"

"Yeah, pretty sure. I bet you wish you went with me to get lunch."

"Lunch? You saw what I saw, right? It wasn't some hallucination, right? Right?"

"What are you talking about?"

"The missing stuff? The words written in blood on the wall? Any of this ring a bell?"

"I really don't know what you're talking about. I was stuck on Highway 59 since noon."

"No, you were there. I know you were," Leyla said. Her head began pounding harder.

"Leyla, just rest now. We'll talk about it later."

Leyla closed her eyes. How could it not have happened? The eerie shadow was real. She knew it.

Leyla spent the next day in the hospital. She went back to her office after being released. Raina strongly advised her not to go, but Leyla had to see for herself that it was all just hallucinations.

As she entered the room, the false memories flooded her mind. Leyla searched for the black light, but couldn't find it. She went to a nearby store and bought one. Retracing her steps, Leyla turned the lights off and pulled down the shade. She switched on the black light. Shining it all around the room, she replied, "It's gone. All the words are gone." She couldn't believe it.

After Raina turned the light on, she replied, "Leyla, I don't think you're going to find what you're looking for. You should get your deposit back and find another space."

No gas leak was ever found. Leyla knew her experience couldn't have been just a hallucination. It was something more. Something supernatural. Leyla knew she should take Raina's advice and give up the space, but she couldn't. She felt there was a piece missing. The place to find answers was on the walls of that room. Somewhere among those words lay the key to unlocking the secret, and Leyla determined to do everything she could to discover it.

Natural Compensation

Mike Massey

"I'm sorry, okay? I don't know where we are." He stared at the map.

"Come on, you're the mapmaker. Don't tell me you can't read one."

"Just give me a minute, Ronny. I'm still looking." His brow furrowed as he traced the roads with his finger.

"Don't call me Ronny! You know I hate it."

His friend smiled and went back to the map. Chris Gentry enjoyed the little needles that slipped so easily under his friend's skin. "The road we want must be farther up from where we turned. But, this road isn't it. I can't even find it on here."

"There's a surprise." Ron gestured back the way they had come. "This road was made and forgotten long before anyone even had maps."

"Give me a break, " said Chris. "All we have to do is go back to where we turned onto this road. That's where we made our mistake."

"I made the mistake when I handed you the map."

"And you've never been lost before?"

"At least when I get lost it's in a place that can be found on a map." Ron went around to his door. "We have to get going. It will be dark soon"

Chris folded the map leaving the part he was reading on top, then folded himself back into his seat.

Ron climbed in, slamming the door. After grinding the starter for a few seconds the engine caught. He eased the truck back into motion.

They bumped along for another mile. The only sounds were the whining "granny gear" and the complaining springs. The truck's mirrors barely scraped past the skinny aspens on either side. It was battle scarred by previous encounters with assorted natural obstacles. Mottled splashes of sunlight crept along the bleached out roof and hood. The higher the road climbed, the steeper and narrower it became until it was no more than two narrow trails with weeds growing between them. As aspens gave way to pines their large branches reached out, blocking even the small patches of sunlight, giving a feeling of dusk. Soon they blocked the road, being pushed out of the way by the weary old truck.

"This is insane!" Ron's limited patience was thinning quickly. "I don't remember a road like this. It's already been nearly six miles, and there is nowhere to turn around. Nowhere!"

"Just stay cool." Chris knew Ron could take a situation from bad to terminal in a matter of minutes. They weren't in trouble yet, but nightfall was coming.

"Something has to give soon," said Chris, trying to keep an even tone. "Then we can get going in the right direction."

"What's going to give is the road," snapped Ron. "It's going to give out! And I don't feel like backing all the way down the mountain. That's six miles— more than six miles and in the dark! Why? Because I let you read the damned map, that's why. Then you led us onto a road that isn't even there. Hell, I don't know where it is! All I wanted was to get away for a couple of days and do a little fishing and you lead us…Oh...my...God!" gasped Ron. He stood on the brakes, nearly throwing Chris through the windshield.

"Hey, what the hell are you doing?" screamed Chris. "You could have killed us!"

"Look," said Ron, pointing out the side window.

The trees parted where the road crossed a small saddle at the ridgeline. Before them lay a small, deep valley. Naked granite peaks thrust up on the far side, patches of snow still clinging stubbornly to the higher places. They appeared even larger against the background of the blue-black sky. A thick blanket of pines covered the lower slopes and valley like a deep shag carpet. At the bottom of the valley a small kidney-shaped lake lay nestled about a mile long, its surface so calm it reflected with the clarity of a fine mirror.

They sat for several minutes looking at the lake, then at each other, then back at the lake.

"Do you still want to turn around?" asked Chris.

"No…I think this deserves a closer look."

Ron slipped the truck into gear and started down into the valley. The forest was as thick on this side of the hill as the one they just came up. The road curved through several tight switchbacks as it descended, following the contour of the hill, finally widening into a lush grassy meadow.

"Well, Toto, I don't think we're in Kansas anymore," said Chris.

The meadow was lined with the same thick stand of pines and scrub. The road traced around the edge then plunged back into the forest. It continued in a gentle curve, ending in a small clearing that opened onto the shore of the lake.

Shutting off the engine, Ron sat back and listened to the silence broken only by the occasional birdsong. Somewhere in the distance a frog croaked. There was not even the hint of a breeze.

A semicircle about two-hundred feet wide covered by short, thick grass pushed up against a narrow strip of pearly white sand on the lakeshore. Circular ripples disturbed the lake's glassy surface as an occasional fish surfaced to snag some insect with the misfortune of flying too low. Long shadows stretched slowly across the tiny valley as the sun slid down behind the ragged peaks.

"This looks like a good place," Ron said quietly. "I think we should stay here."

"Yeah," said Chris. "I just wish I knew where 'here' was."

They set up the tent with a small fire pit a few feet in front of it. Chris sat at the shore fishing. Nothing was biting yet but, with the sun down, that was bound to change soon.

Ron went off in search of firewood. "If we're going to eat fish," he said, "we're going to cook them over a real campfire, not a camp stove. Some things just shouldn't be compromised."

Stars were already appearing when he returned, so he wasted no time getting a fire going. Ron gathered a fair-sized armload of wood, but there didn't seem to be very much to be had. There was enough for tonight, but that was all.

As he rummaged through the boxes, unpacking cooking utensils and spices, he felt the hair stand up on the back of his neck. Turning, he expected to see Chris standing there. Instead, the shadow of a horse and a very large man stood in the shadows just inside the tree line.

"Hey, buddy," he called. There was a slight tremor in his voice. "Can I help you with something?"

The stranger strode slowly out of the shadows, seeming to grow taller as he approached. Ron shook his head to clear his vision. Well over six feet tall with a physique that would make a linebacker jealous, the man was enormous with long black hair in braids dangling over his shoulders. Leather buckskins and knee high moccasins completed the strange image.

Regaining his usual cockiness, Ron called, "Hey, Chris, we've got company."

Turning back to the Indian, "Yo! Sitting Bull, or whatever your name is, you gonna say something or just stand there eyeballing me all night?"

"How did you come to this place?" The man spoke softly but the rumble in his voice carried an ominous tone, as if he was accustomed to people listening when he spoke.

"We came in a truck," said Ron, laughing.

"How did you come to this place?"

"I don't think he's into your jokes," said Chris as he came to stand by his friend, a stringer of large trout in his grip.

The Indian eyed Chris and the stringer, then turned back to Ron.

"Okay," said Ron, "We got lost, and this is where we ended up. Do you have a problem with that?"

"This is sacred land."

"Sacred land?" Chris grinned. He tossed the fish onto the tailgate of the truck. "I don't know anything about sacred land, but I do know a killer fishing hole when I see one. And this is one KILLER fishing hole."

"Long ago this land was set aside by the Gods. It is sacred land."

"Well, that explains it for me," said Ron. "Listen, I'd really like to hear more about this sacred land bit, but I'm hungry. I don't think my friend would mind if you joined us, would you?" He looked at Chris who smiled nervously and shrugged. "Then you can tell us about your sacred lands."

The Indian nodded slightly and said, "I will stay."

"By the way," said Ron, "We don't even know your name."

"I am called Red Claw," he said.

Ron cocked his head and crinkled his forehead, "Interesting name. Must have some kind of meaning to it." Picking up a knife, he cleaned and cooked the fish while Chris peeled and fried some potatoes. They all ate heartily.

Through the entire meal Red Claw said nothing. When they finished, he went to his horse and brought back a water bag, a small pouch and a long object with a tassel of feathers on it.

Ron and Chris settled next to the fire with some beer. When Chris offered one to their guest he waved it off. They looked at each other for a moment. "He doesn't drink beer."

They sat quietly, letting their meal settle while the Indian fiddled with his pouch and the long object. It didn't occur to either of them until he drew a burning twig from the fire that it was a pipe he prepared. Ron gave Chris a sly grin. He had heard all the wild rumors about what Indians smoked in their peace pipes but had never been able to find out for himself.

Red Claw lit the pipe and took a deep drag before passing it over to Ron. He had smoked marijuana before, but as Ron took a drag from the pipe he realized it was like nothing he had ever tasted. Chris took a small drag and tried not to look undignified by coughing. He handed the pipe quickly back to the Indian who took another puff then sent it around again. The next time Chris handed it to him, he set it aside.

"Now," said Ron, "I believe we're ready to hear about your sacred land." He started to feel considerably mellower and a little lightheaded. He also noticed his usual sarcasm wasn't so quick to surface, and he didn't really care. "Must be what was in the pipe," he thought.

Red Claw waited a moment, then he began, "Long ago there was a great medicine man. He was called Slow Wolf. When the white man drove his people from the land there was great suffering. It was winter, and many became sick with fever and died as they were forced from one place to another. There was little he could do for them. There was not enough food or medicine.

"Slow Wolf also became sick with fever. For many days he slept the sleep of the dead. As he slept one of the Gods came to him and showed him a vision of the future. He saw the white man killing and driving his people till there were few left. He saw them kill off many animals. He saw forests that were home to the eagle and the bear cut down and burned away to make room for the white man's villages and farms. The Gods showed him many terrible things that were poured into the rivers and lakes by huge houses. Fish no longer swam there. Animals died when they drank the water. Soon the rivers were also silent."

"White men of great power lived in the villages. People who had nothing also lived in these places. Sometimes they starved to death."

"Slow Wolf asked how these things could be. How could people with so much power live with plenty and leave others within their own cities to die with nothing. Why would they destroy the forests and animals that the Gods gave to us as gifts?"

"The Gods told Slow Wolf this was the way of the white man. The white man gained power by destroying things that got in his way. Slow Wolf and his people were one of those things. For the white man to feel strong another must be weaker. This was their unspoken law."

"Slow Wolf asked if all the land and water must be defiled this way, if the Gods could save just a small piece of land from the white man's sorrow."

"They said it was not yet time for Slow Wolf to die. When that time came, they would return and guide Slow Wolf to a place in the mountains. This place would be protected, and the white man would not come there. Slow Wolf would be the keeper of the land."

"The God left Slow Wolf and, in time, the fever left him."

"The white man moved Slow Wolf and his people onto a reservation. They kept them like animals. Many more died. No more were they the people who rode upon the wide plains and hunted the buffalo.

"Many years later the Gods returned to Slow Wolf and told him it was time to go to the land that was promised. No person would be able to find this place. It would remain as it was when Slow Wolf came. The Gods said he should not be alone. He gave him a horse as a companion and a great bear as protector. Slow Wolf walks these hills and drinks and fishes from this lake. It will be this way until the Gods return to burn all the people from the earth and take back the land."

"Well," said Ron, "I don't see what this has to do with us."

"You have come onto sacred land. Only the Gods could allow you to come here." His voice took on an ominous tone, "But be warned, use only what you need from this land. Kill only what you will eat while you are here. Take nothing from this place and leave nothing. This land is living. It breathes, and it feels. Beware, the Keeper. Harm this land, and he will do whatever he must to make right that which is wrong.

Red Claw rose and strode quickly to his horse. "Beware, the Keeper. He will protect this land." With agility that belied his size, he hopped onto his horse and was soundlessly gone.

"That was weird, "said Ron. "Their old folks must sit around the campfire all night and make up these wild stories. Then they tell them to the white men hoping it will scare them off." He took another beer from the cooler. "He can tell his stories, but he's not going to scare off this white man."

94

"You know, Ron, "These stories have to start from some kind of fact, even if it doesn't seem that way."

"You don't believe all that crap, do you?"

"Of course not, but we need to keep an eye out for this guy in case he comes back again."

"I think he made up that sacred land story to run a couple of white folks from what he considers his private game preserve."

The next morning dawned clear and cold. A light breeze rippled the surface of the lake. The sound of birds completed a peaceful scene. Chris was the first to waken. He quickly pulled on his boots and crawled out of the tent. At this altitude it was always cold early in the morning. Pulling on his jacket, he walked down to the lakeshore. This was always his favorite part of the day when he camped. The early sun, low in the sky, combining with the crisp chill seemed to give everything a sense of sharper contrast.

He knelt and splashed water on his face.

He and his older brother, Brian, grew up on their Uncle's farm in Ohio. During the summer, after they finished their chores, they would spend the rest of their day at the pond on the "back forty". It was fed by an underground spring, making the water very cold. A huge oak tree growing on one side stretched out over the water, a tire swing hanging from one of its branches. Chris loved the rush of that first breathless chill he would get after plunging into the icy water. He would quickly swim to shore and stand shivering like a wet puppy in the summer sun. After he warmed up, he'd do it all over again.

Ron wakened to bacon sizzling and the smell of fresh coffee in the air. He could not be called a morning person. As he crawled out of the tent, Chris could see he was going to have a harder than usual time getting started. They had been camping and fishing partners since high school. Unlike Chris, Ron was always slow in the morning. Chris usually took care of getting coffee and breakfast started. They had been doing this for so long it was now routine.

Ron wandered bleary-eyed to the fire. "Is it battery acid yet?"

"Yeah, don't burn yourself. Cups are still in the box."

He wandered to the truck and rummaged through the back till he found the cups. "You can just hook me up to the pot. I'll take it intravenously." He went back and sat next to the fire.

They made quick work of breakfast. After the dishes were washed they sat by the fire with their coffee, waiting for the air to warm.

"I think a little exploring would be a good idea," said Chris. "Find out what the fishing is like on the other side of the lake. Who knows? Maybe there is a trophy sitting out there, just waiting for someone to pull him in."

"And you believe that you're just that someone. Always the optimistic one, aren't you?" Ron grinned over his cup. "One day Moby Dick is going to come and swallow you up. We'll see how that affects your confidence level."

"Yeah, right," Chris answered. "You're just jealous you're not the one that catches the big ones." He threw the rest of his coffee onto the fire. "I can gather more firewood on the way back."

"Do you really think there's enough wood there for another night? You don't know how far I had to go to get what we had."

"Don't you think that's a bit odd? We're surrounded by forest and yet there's no dead wood lying around? So, what do you suggest?"

"I could cut something down." said Ron.

"Okay. Just make it something small, we don't need a bonfire."

Ron sized up the trees around the clearing. "I'll deal with the firewood problem. If you feel like exploring, go for it. My head still hurts from our little party last night."

"I thought you were whispering because you didn't want to wake the squirrels." Chris got up, grinning. "I'll be back in awhile." he said, and disappeared into the trees.

Ron watched him go, then turned back to the problem at hand. He knew freshly cut wood did not burn very well. There would be a lot of smoke and popping, but since it was all they had, it's what they would use. He dug the chain saw from the back of the truck and checked the fuel.

Choosing a tree was difficult. They all seemed to have unusually large trunks. He picked one about fifteen feet tall. After getting the saw started, he set himself for the first cut. He drew back suddenly as a chill gripped his stomach. The bark on the tree seemed to shrunk back from the blade. He stood for a moment, stunned. Chuckling, he chided himself for his foolishness. Plants didn't move— not on their own.

He brought the saw up again and saw the bark pulling away from the rushing blade. Not giving in to the chill this time, he set his jaw and let the blade gnaw into the pale wood, the engine howling like a savage predator. The forest around him gave an audible sigh as the blade bit deeper into the tree. Icy fingers crept into his bowels and up

96

his spine. Grimly, he continued to cut, pulling the blade free and slicing in at another angle to take out a wedge. A crack like a pistol shot signaled the last section of wood giving way. With a groan the tree slowly toppled over. The trunk twisted slowly, and a large branch stretched out, reaching toward him as it fell. He ducked as it whistled past him, missing by a mere fraction of an inch.

He stood back for a moment to settle his nerves. That was close! He was sure his mind was playing tricks on him. Trees did not reach for things. He revved the saw again and trimmed off the branches, stacking them out of the way, then cut the trunk into smaller sections.

Halfway up its length, a sudden explosion of movement flew out of the log into his face. Crying out, he fell backward, dropping the saw. The sound of wings beating the air drew his attention to a large owl climbing away from him. It must have been trapped in its nest inside the tree and escaped when he rolled the log over.

Dusting himself off, he sat on the stump.

•

Chris hadn't gone far before he found the trace of a game trail. In some places he needed to duck to avoid low hanging branches. He heard an occasional rustle of leaves or twigs as a bird would take to wing, or some other small creature would scurry back to the safety of its den. The path skirted the perimeter of the lake. That was good. It meant there was less chance of getting lost. Getting lost was the last thing that he wanted in a place like this.

He had gone only about a quarter of a mile before he came upon a row of huge, flat-topped boulders. Time and weather had worn them smooth. Several bore long cracks where water had seeped into crevices and frozen, splitting them as cleanly as any stonemason could.

He chose one that jutted several yards out into the lake and sat where he could get the best view.

All around the lake an unbroken blanket of trees came right down to the shore and extended up to the rim of the valley where they met the sky. Chris could not remember seeing a forest so dense. It appeared to be a solid thing.

The lake was as calm as on the previous day. The water barely moved around the great rocks, and he was astonished at how clear it was. He could see several feet down to smooth grasses and bushy water plants swaying in the currents. Off to the left he noticed a muddy green log partially buried beneath the grass.

Chris gazed silently into the water, almost hypnotized by the gentle swaying of the plants on the bottom. With a start, his attention was jerked away by a movement a few feet away.

He mentally kicked himself for not bringing any fishing gear. Here was a school of trout, the largest of which must have weighed several pounds. He watched in amazement as they milled around, occasionally surfacing to snatch an unwary insect. The sunlight threw brilliant reflections off smooth, silvery scales as their sleek bodies moved effortlessly through the crystal water. It was like watching something from a nature film.

Chris was ready to go back and retrieve his fishing gear when a giant swirl in the surface obscured the view below. His pulse suddenly leaped, and his heart knotted in surprise. This wasn't the kind of ripple the trout were making. He waited for the water to settle so he could see what was there. He saw was nothing. The trout were gone, as if something had scared them off. Whatever it was must have left with them.

He scanned the water looking for the telltale ripples of feeding trout. Only the log was still there. Another chill gripped him. The log had moved! He knew there were currents under the water but there was no evidence of anything strong enough to move something the size of that log. Yet, it was several feet from where he had first seen it.

As he looked closer, he realized there was something wrong with it. Then, to his amazement, it flexed and moved off several feet. His eyes flew open wide. "Holy cow!" he exclaimed to himself. "This is no log. It's a trophy-sized fish."

Chris got down closer to the water to get a better look and figure out what kind of fish it was so he could decide the best way to catch it. He was taking that fish home with him!

It didn't have the sparkling scales of the trout he had seen. In fact, it didn't have any scales at all. His mind flashed through a mental catalog, trying to decide what fit the description of the monster in the water.

It shifted slightly revealing a gleaming red eye. He could make out a definite shape in the body. It looked like a giant catfish. He had heard of them growing to phenomenal sizes, but he thought those were just flukes or creative fish stories. He grinned as he thought of something his uncle once said. "I don't know if all fishermen are liars or all liars are fishermen. But, I do know that you won't meet one that doesn't have at least one whopping good fish tale for you."

His uncle had taught him to fish. He also taught him the art of telling a good fish story. And Uncle Grant had plenty of whopping good fish tales. This was at least five feet of whopping good fish tale, and it was going to hang on his wall if he had anything to say about it.

The only thing that bothered him was that he didn't think you could find catfish in cold mountain lakes like this one. "It must be a mutant or something."

He hopped down from the rock and headed back the way he came. It really didn't matter where it had come from. It was here now, and he was going to do his best to catch it. And if he didn't, it would be a story he wouldn't tell anyone. Hopefully, it would stay put till he got back.

Sprinting down the trail as fast as the growth would allow him, he almost clothes-lined himself on a low hanging branch.

He burst into camp, narrowly missing a large heap of pine boughs. Ron sat close by on a stump. The trunk of a tree was cut into sections to split into firewood.

Chris pulled his tackle box from the back of the truck and started digging through another box.

"What's going on?" asked Ron.

"A catfish. A real big catfish." He crawled out of the truck with a large coil of clothesline, still out of breath as he started to dig through his tackle box. Finally, in frustration, he dumped it onto the ground.

Ron became curious. "Are you sure the altitude isn't starting to affect your brain functions just a little bit?" He came over to watch but kept a respectable distance. "Maybe a little hyperventilation would be a good idea to get some oxygen back into those brain cells."

"Right," said Chris. "What do think I've been doing? Holding my breath?"

"Well, running through the forest like a madman with his ass on fire over some fish is not your usual way of doing things. What else is going on?"

"Look, Ron, this is not just some fish. This is a catfish that must be at least five feet long, maybe more." He found two huge hooks and set them aside, then scooped everything back into the box. "I'm going back down to that spot, and I'm going to pull that thing out of the water. I may need your help."

"You may need my help." Ron chuckled. "Chris, if you say there's a giant catfish in this lake, I want to be there to see you pull it out. I don't think you're going to find anything but trout in these waters."

"That's okay. This lake isn't on the map either. I don't care if you come to watch or just laugh at me, so long as you're there to help if I need it." He put all the things he gathered into a small canvas bag, grabbed his fishing pole, and headed for the trees. "Are you coming?"

Chris set a fast pace. Ron kept losing sight of him through the trees. Ducking low hanging branches didn't help.

"Hey!"

Ron stopped short, startled by the voice.

"This is the place."

He looked around for the source of the voice. Chris sat on a huge boulder. Shaking his head, Ron climbed up next to him. "Damn, what a view."

"The fish is still there." said Chris, pointing down at a dark form on the bottom of the lake.

"That's a log," Said Ron. "You brought me all the way out here just to see a log?"

"Just sit here and watch a minute. Tell me if you see it do anything." Chris backed down the boulder to a spot that became relatively level and dumped everything out of the bag.

"Now what are you doing?"

"Just stay up there and watch that thing. I'm going to show you how to catch a log."

He tied one end of a narrow cord to a tree and went farther back to another tree, wrapping the cord around it. Then, picking up his bait and hooks, he climbed back onto the rock and sat down.

"Anything move down there yet?"

"Nope. Want to explain what you're doing?"

"Not yet. Better hold your nose. This smells real bad. I bought this stuff a few weeks ago and haven't had a chance try it yet."

The smell hit them as soon as the cover was off.

Ron covered his nose. "Aw man, that stuff would knock a buzzard off a shit-wagon. How long has it been dead?"

Chris scooped out a big gob and packed it around the hook. "To catfish, this is like chocolate cake."

100

"Man, if my mother made a chocolate cake that smelled like that my dad would have thrown her out with it."

"You wouldn't make a very good catfish, either." Chris lowered the hook into the water. "Now we wait."

The forest became quiet, as if all the birds and animals held their breath.

The strike was so quick that it startled both of them. The log moved like lightning snatching the bait, then settled back to the bottom and spit out the empty hook.

The men looked at each other, then back at the fish. Chris drew the hook up out of the water. "He must have felt some bare metal or something."

He dug out a bigger gob of bait this time and packed the hook again, then lowered it into the water. They watched as it settled to the bottom. It had no sooner touched than, in a swirl of water, the big fish snatched it up again. When he settled back down the cord trailed from his mouth.

"You going to set the hook?" asked Ron.

"Nope, you saw how fast he spit it out. I'm going to let him swallow it this time."

Soon another section of line was drawn into the water. "I think we have him now." Chris slowly pulled in the line. The fish allowed them to turn him toward the rock, then took off for deeper water.

"Stay clear of that line," Chris warned. "There's about a hundred feet, and he'll probably take all of it."

The line hummed as it ran out over the edge of the rock, then came to the end with a loud snap! Leaves fell as the tree quivered from the shock. The line twitched as the fish fought, but it held.

Ron turned, grinning, "Now that you have him, what are you going to do with him?"

"You stay up here and watch that line." He tossed Ron a pair of gloves from the pile, "Put these on. You'll need them." He ran down to where the line passed around the tree and started to pull it in, hand over hand, using the tree as a pulley. The fish, finding itself dragged in a direction it did not want to go, began to fight harder than ever.

"You have him up to the rock," called Ron.

"Okay. Now you have to help me pull him up out of the water."

"How am I supposed to do that without getting stabbed?" Ron looked back at his friend like he had just asked him to jump in after the fish.

"Just be careful. If you can get his head up over the edge of the rock we can drag him the rest of the way up."

"So you say. If this doesn't work you'll be dragging both of us back up."

Ron squatted on the edge of the rock, grabbed the struggling fish by the bottom jaw, and began to lift him up out of the water. Sensing that he was being dragged onto dry land, the fish began to fight with a vengeance. Twice Ron was almost pulled into the water, but Chris jerked the line hard enough to pull him back from the edge.

Finally, he reached the spine on the fish's back. When he got a good hold he pulled hard, putting all of his weight behind it. He fell backward onto the rock, pulling the fish on top. Scrambling out from under it, he nearly got his face raked by one of its spines. It slid down the rock and onto the grass where it lay still flopping hard.

"You okay, Ron?" Chris leaned against a tree trying to catch his breath.

"Yeah, I'm okay. I always did want to wrestle a two-hundred pound catfish." The fish made a throaty croaking sound. "Oh, shut up." He threw his gloves at it. "Now that we have it, what do we do next? I've seen these things live for hours out of the water."

"That's easy." said Chris. He picked up a large round stone and smacked it down onto the base of the fish's head. The rock made a dull crunching sound. The fish twitched once more and was still.

Chris snapped a tape from his belt and handed one end to Ron. "Let's see how long he is."

He checked it twice when he read it. "I don't believe this."

"Well, tell me so I can not believe it, too."

"How about six feet ten inches."

"You're serious, aren't you?"

"Do you want to hold this end of the tape? Of course I'm serious. This is bigger than any fish I've caught since that shark down in Florida." He re-rolled the tape and started packing up the fishing gear.

"Chris, have you given any thought to how we're going to get this thing back to camp with us?"

"I've already worked that out. We just take down a sapling like that one over there." He said, pointing to a small tree "and lash the fish to it. Then we carry it out like you would pack out a deer."

Chris had a hatchet in the bag with the other things. He put it to good use cutting down the sapling. As he struck it the first time, a shiver ran up his back. "That felt like the whole forest just inhaled," he said softly.

"Try to ignore it," said Ron. "This whole place seems to do that."

Chris didn't say a word but finished cutting down the tree and trimming off the branches. Then they lashed the fish to it. Wrestling the ends of the pole onto their shoulders, they staggered off toward camp.

The going was hard down the narrow trail. They hadn't gone very far when Ron got a strange prickly feeling on the back of his neck. He stopped so quickly that Chris almost walked out from under the front of the pole.

"Hey! What are you doing?" He fought to regain his balance without dropping it.

"Have you ever had the feeling you're being watched?"

They set the fish down, and Ron collapsed onto a large rock, pale and trembling.

"How can we be followed when there isn't anyone around here but us," asked Chris.

"What about that Indian whats-his-name and his bear?"

"Oh, come on. Campfire legends to scare kids, women and white men."

"Yeah, you said that before. But what if there are bears around here? This is the right kind of country."

"Well, if there are, and we're not sure, I don't think sitting around the woods with a six foot fish is the smartest way to find out."

The last stretch into camp seemed to take an eternity. They crouched low to get under branches, and it got harder to straighten after each one. Their arms, shoulders and backs burned from the strain. When they finally arrived at the camp they rolled the fish to the ground and collapsed next to it.

After several minutes Ron pulled himself up and sat against a tree. "How much do you think it weighs?"

"Probably more than either of us," said Chris.

"I think we should find someplace to stash him, or we may not keep him very long."

"Are you afraid the bears will come and get him?"

"You never can tell."

"You still jumpy?" asked Chris.

"There was something out there. You're just not going to believe it unless you see it."

"Uh huh. Let's just roll this guy up in a tarp and put him into the back of the truck. That way, if, and I say IF there is a bear out there, he won't have such an easy time getting to it."

Ron dug the tarp out, and after moving some things around they slid the bundle into the space.

"Have a beer?" asked Ron. He produced two bottles dripping ice water from the cooler.

"Yeah." Chris felt his ribs and head. "I wonder if this is how a marathon runner feels after a race."

Ron tossed the bottle to him, then motioned to the pile of branches. "Do you have any suggestions for dealing with that?"

"Tonight we celebrate. We can cook the fish that's left over. Then we'll build ourselves a great big bonfire."

When sunset came a bonfire roared in the center of the camp. Ron and Chris sat on the tailgate, beer in hand, watching the sun go down. A slight breeze rippled on the surface of the lake.

"Have another beer," asked Ron, reaching into the cooler.

"Just hold onto it for a minute." Chris got up and disappeared around the front of the truck. There was an anxious look on his face when he returned. "There's something big out there, and it's checking out the camp. I could hear it moving in the trees."

"Hearing bears in the forest, huh? Maybe we should go out and see if we can find them."

"You know, Ron, sometimes you're crazier than I act. Why don't we just tie steaks around our necks?"

"Now who's the jumpy one? I was only joking. Besides, I forgot the steaks."

"Well, I'm not hearing things, and I'm not joking, but I am tired. I really hate to break up this party but I need some sleep." Chris chugged the rest of his beer and tossed his bottle into the fire, sending a huge cloud of sparks into the air.

"Watch out for the bears." His voice dripped sarcasm. Then he ducked into the tent.

"Watch out for bears." Ron chuckled to himself. "They aren't going to come near this fire."

He finished the beer and tossed the bottle into the fire then watched the sparks rush skyward. After looking around, he stood and relieved himself into the fire. "This one is for Smokey-the-bear!" he shouted to the fire. Laughing, he got another beer and leaned back against the cooler, staring into the fire.

He knew he would have to sleep soon. The hard day and the beer were having their affect on him. He would just sit a while longer...

Ron woke with a start, shivering violently. Shaking his head, he tried to remember where he was. A small slice of moon dimly lit the campsite. A single flame in a large circle of ashes marked where the bonfire had been. He saw his half-finished beer lying next to the fish.

Something wasn't right. His head pounded, and he could not figure out what it was. The beer..? THE FISH! Suddenly, he was wide awake. They had rolled the fish in a tarp and put it into the back of the truck. Now, it was lying on the ground, the tarp in a heap beside it. A bloody hole gaped open where the dorsal spine had been.

Panic stricken, he looked around, wildly searching for some clue to what was going on. He almost missed the very old, white-haired Indian sitting on the ground on the far side of the dying bonfire singing softly to himself.

Suddenly, Ron's panic was replaced by intense rage. "What the hell are you doing here?" he screamed as he stomped around to the old man, his headache now forgotten.

"You do not heed the warnings from Red Claw," Said the old man. His voice sounded as brittle as he looked.

"Screw your warnings!" Ron shouted, reaching for him. A huge hand closed over his shoulder, and he felt himself flying away from the old man.

"Do not touch the Keeper" said Red Claw.

Ron staggered back to his feet. He hadn't realized how huge this man really was. And quiet! Where did he come from?

"You have offended the forest. You kill what you do not eat. You destroy the trees. You do not care about the land.

"What's going on out here?" Chris came crawling out of the tent.

"The Gods are angered. The sins against the land must be repaid."

"If you're so upset about it," said Ron, "why don't you just take the fish, and we'll leave. We promise we won't come back."

"It is not so easy as this," said the Keeper. "The sins must be repaid." He slowly got to his feet and picked up a long staff that had lain unnoticed on the ground. Strange looking runes were carved into its entire length. Then he raised his hands and the staff into the air and began to chant and dance slowly in a small circle. The staff began to glow a dull orange.

"Now what do you think you're doing," asked Ron. He started toward the Indian again. "I'm about tired of this crap. This joke is over NOW, buddy!"

The old man turned and glared at him, stopping him in his tracks. He tried to take another step but couldn't move.

"Ron, what did he do to your truck?" Ron spun around to see blistered paint flaking off, exposing dull orange rust. The colors of the interior began to fade as cracks appeared in the leather seats. It seemed to be aging several years in a matter of seconds. One of the tires exploded like a gunshot making both of them jump. A cloud of reddish dust puffed up as that corner of the truck settled then collapsed.

Ron was shaken out of his shock and lunged at the old Indian. "I'm going to kill you, you son-of-a..."

He heard a twig snap, and something slammed into his left side sending a white hot flash of pain through his arm and shoulder right before he crashed into a tree. Dazed, he slid to the ground, feeling as if he was watching himself from a distance. He blinked once, trying to clear his pain fogged vision.

When he looked up he was staring into the baleful eyes of Red Claw. With the fluidity of a dream the Indian's face seemed to transform into that of a huge bear. He let out a loud angry roar, his hot breath stinking of old meat and blood. Ron felt his bladder let go. When he opened his eyes he was looking into the face of the giant Indian again.

The Keeper's voice came from somewhere behind Red Claw. "You have felt fear. Soon you will know despair. You will know it as you know a lover. Soon, but the time is not yet."

Chris watched in stunned silence. Now, the old Indian turned to him. "From both of you, the land will have what is due. As the Gods have spoken, so shall it be."

106

He took a long object from his belt. Chris realized it was the missing spine from the catfish; about 18 inches long and very sharp. The Indian raised his arms wide and began to sing in the chanting rhythm again. The spine and staff began to glow like they were suddenly white-hot.

He backed up as the old Indian slowly advanced on him. "He told you that you could have the fish."

Chris was almost in tears by this time. "I don't really want it now, anyway. We'll just leave, and we promise to never come back, ever. We'll just leave here, and you'll never see us a…" He fell backwards over one of the cut logs.

At that moment Red Claw stepped around the old man and took the glowing spine from his hand. In one fluid movement he dropped to one knee and drove the spine deep into Chris's chest.

Chris felt as if he had been shot through with fire. He felt himself being lifted from the ground as he stared at the thing protruding from his chest. Red Claw propped him against a tree, then with the palm of his hand he slammed the spine hard the rest of the way through his body. Hearing a crunching sound as it slid out between his shoulder blades, Chris' whole world flashed in a blaze of flaming, red agony. In the distance he heard someone screaming. Was it him? He couldn't feel his legs anymore. Each breath was like gasping molten lava into his lungs. His mind raced, trying to grasp some small piece of reality. His unbelieving eyes watched as his nerveless fingers scrabbled at the short stump protruding from his chest.

"The land will keep you, and you will become the land." Red Claw stepped back as the Keeper poked the bony stump with his staff.

Chris felt the sensation of tiny insects crawling on his chest. It began to spread over his body causing him to sweat, coating him in a slimy mess. He watched unbelieving as his clothes dissolved, and the skin of his legs drew together till they became one limb. He screamed again in pain as his feet flattened into a round vertical fin.

Ron was still sitting against the tree grasping his left arm. In stunned silence, he watched his friend's arms draw shorter and shorter till there were just long thin bones sticking out from the sides of his body. His fingers elongated, becoming webbed fins attached to the bones. Another fin slowly grew up the length of the spine protruding from his back.

Chris looking around, blind panic in his voice. 'Ron, you have to stop him!" he screamed. "Don't let them do this to me! They're going to kill you, too!"

The Keeper chanted louder.

Chris' head flattened out as his eyes slowly moved over to each side. His neck disappeared, drawing his head back to his shoulders. Large gill slits opened on either side. His screams gurgled into throaty croaks. He flopped around weakly, his gills fanning open and closed.

Red Claw lifted him effortlessly over one shoulder and carried him down to the lake. He stood for a moment, then threw him into the water.

Free of his load, he turned and stared at Ron. "Now," he said, "You will know true despair."

In a panic, Ron tried to stand. The movement sent a new jolt of pain through his left side. He gasped for breath as his vision faded to gray for a moment before he forced himself the rest of the way up. The Keeper slowly advanced on him.

"Stay away from me." Ron hissed through clenched teeth.

He turned to run and felt a huge paw slap him across the back of his knees, shattering one of them. He fell again, screaming, as his world started to slip away into unconsciousness.

He was being lifted back onto his feet as something ran down his face and into his eyes, burning as it went. When he opened his eyes Red Claw's face was mere inches from his own. The Keeper was standing behind Ron pouring something from a leather bag over his head. His vision blurred, and he thought he saw the face in front of him going from that of a man to a bear, back to a man, flickering like some kind of ancient movie. His mind raced as clarity finally struck him…a giant bear, Red Claw? Red Claw was the bear!

Ron's skin felt very dry and itchy all over his body. He tried to move but his joints were growning stiff. He looked down and saw his clothes swelling into thick crusty ridges.

"What are you doing to me?" He tried to get away, but he couldn't move his feet. He looked down to see small tendrils breaking out through his shoes and sliding into the ground like roots securing him to the spot. "Why are you doing this to me? I didn't do anything!" His screams were swallowed by the forest.

The Keeper's voice was calm, "You have defiled sacred land. You have killed what you will not eat and destroyed what you will not use.

Red Claw brought you the warning. You have chosen not to listen. Now the land must be repaid.

"NO!" Ron lashed out with his good arm. Red Claw caught it effortlessly. He watched as crusty ridges crept up the arm. The fingers stretched and split apart like thin branches. His other arm hung dry and broken at his side.

Ron stared at the old Indian through shock-glazed eyes. "Who are you?"

The old man smiled. "I am the Keeper." He dumped the rest of the bag's contents over Ron's head and face. Red Claw is the bear the God's gave me as protection and a companion.

Ron's long scream finally ended as flesh became wood and bark, leaving a small gnarled tree with a broken branch hanging from the left side. An odd-shaped hole with strange curls around it showed where his mouth and face had been.

Around the clearing were small ragged piles of debris, all that was left of the camping gear. Black slime marked where the fish had been. The split wood was neatly stacked on a travois behind the horse.

The Keeper looked out across the lake at gathering clouds. Beneath them, the world was becoming unusually dark. Lightning lanced down giving the darkness under the clouds a surreal appearance. Wind whipped the lake into a froth.

At the sound of the distant thunder a faint smile crept across his face. He spread his arms wide as if to welcome the advancing storm, the cleansing storm. Then, turning away from the lake, he pulled the broken branch from the tree and tossed it into the remains of fire. He walked off into the forest, leading the horse, followed by Red Claw.

The clouds gathered quickly, their shadows racing across the lake. The sun was blotted out, giving the appearance of dusk. As the lightning came closer, blue-white flashes lit the landscape brighter than day. Darkness filled in, deeper than ever.

The rolling thunder sent a tremor through the ground. Another started the trees vibrating. The ground beneath the truck began to settle, deeper and deeper.

A few large drops fell. Then, all at once the rain became a torrential downpour. The thunder was muted by the sound of falling rain. A hole opened steadily larger beneath the truck. Water drained into it in tiny rivulets that grew larger as the rain came harder.

Another bolt of lightning struck only scant feet away. The ground hissed as the mud and water boiled instantly into steam. A rumble began deep in the earth. The puddle under the truck disappeared as the bottom of the hole fell away. Each new roll of thunder opened it wider. The truck continued to sink. Soon only the front bumper was visible. With one last, convulsive shudder it, too, disappeared.

The morning dawned bright on the tiny lake. A light breeze pushed small puffy clouds across a deep blue sky. In a grassy clearing on the shore, a small bird was beginning to build a nest in a short gnarled tree. The bird didn't remember the tree being there before, but it had an opening that made an ideal spot for a nest. A few feet away lay a large muddy depression with a pool of water in the center. After the water cleared it would be a good place to bathe and splash, safe from the giant fish that lurked just off the shore. Yes, it was an ideal spot for a nest.

Shades Of Gray

We say nothing is absolute
In this enlightened time,
Morality is destitute
And not much is a crime
We fail to see what's wrong or right
Through conscience clouded haze –
We've done away with black and white
And substituted grays.

How easily the untrained eye
Sees white blend into gray
An extra drop or two of dye
And black's not far away.
Subtle differences in shade
Require a contrast stark
Next to black dull gray will fade
 And not appear so dark.

Now contrast that same muted tone
Against a crisp white shirt
Its darkness then is clearly shown
To be a smudge of dirt.
But many will avert their eyes
And thus ignore the grime –
Or choose to don a gray disguise
And blend in with the slime.

The stuff composing all our brains –
Gray matter to be sure –
By our own choosing oft refrains
From being clean and pure.
What we put in is manifest
By what we say and do
Our actions, be they cursed or blessed
From our gray matter grew.

We seem content to live in gray
With colours all around
Why do we into darkness stray
When light can still be found?
I see the world in black and white
And multi-coloured hues –
Some things are wrong and some are right
And grays I will refuse.

By Sharon Kasenberg

Acceptance

C. L. Scarr

Luke "Eagle Eye" Tanner strolled along the beach bordering the Gulf of Aden. Long ago this area had been a popular tourist destination. What had once been a near-paradise now languished in disrepair and ruin. But he wasn't here on vacation. He wasn't interested in plush accommodations or improving his tan. He was here to pay tribute. It was July 23rd, an anniversary he honored every year by returning to this spot, the place where Marian had died.

Today, five years later, the faint stirrings of an emotion other than anger were beginning to grow. Luke savored the feeling of sand between his toes, noticed the whisper of breeze flowing through palm branches overhead. Two gulls squawked and shrilled on the beach ahead of him, fighting over some dead morsel. He stooped to pick up a piece of driftwood and tossed it into the waves.

Now, he found that he could stand to look back on the happier times. He remembered how Marian had looked the first time he saw her. Long, slender legs alternately hidden and exposed as the wind played with the white gauzy shift she wore over her bikini. Dark waist-length hair tied back with a blue ribbon. Eyes alight with laughter.

He'd been on shore leave in Hawaii. She was a local newspaper reporter on her day off. He knew the moment he saw her that he wanted to get to know her. He struck up a conversation, and they found they had much in common. They spent the rest of his leave time together. But then he had to ship out again.

He kept in touch, calling and writing her often. Ambitious and very good at her job, she moved on to work for a national paper soon after they met. Within a year, she got a job at CNN and worked her way up to a position as foreign correspondent.

They managed to meet from time to time when he was in port. She would take a few days off and fly to wherever he was. They explored each new city together, trying new foods, enjoying local bands. At night, they explored each other.

The first and last time he saw her, she'd been on a beach. The last time was here in Somalia, five years ago today. He and his squad were on patrol up on the road between Saylac and Berbera, not far from where he stood now. The film crew, coming from the other direction, flagged them down.

When Marian hopped out of the CNN jeep, he thought his heart would stop. A giddy delight at seeing her mixed with dread as she started asking questions.

Then they'd been attacked. The ambush caught the patrol standing outside their armored personnel carrier and the film crew outside their Jeep. The soldiers quickly shoved the reporters behind the APC and returned fire. After a brief argument with her cameraman, Marian grabbed the camera and raced to the beach for a better angle. She'd caught some gripping footage before a bullet caught her. His men held off the attackers for over an hour before reinforcements arrived, but they sustained heavy casualties. Luke took rounds to the chest and legs and awoke in the hospital three days later.

After the firefight on the beach and his long recuperation, he'd felt dead inside. He tried using whiskey to erase the memory of that horrible afternoon, and for a few months he thought he might succeed. But when he came back to this place to mark the first anniversary, Luke didn't drink. He sat on the hot sands for hours, staring out at the implacable ocean. At last he admitted that Marian wouldn't have wanted him to go through life as a drunk. The desire to drown the memories still gnawed at him, but he never drank again.

He returned again the following year, and each year after that. He couldn't describe what he was looking for. He knew he'd never have peace of mind. "Closure" was a word women used. The shrink back at the base was a woman and constantly used the word. Maybe acceptance was what he wanted. Needed. If he could just accept what had happened as a fact, without judging or blaming, without the searing pain of heartache, he might have a chance. A chance to start again. A chance to see the goodness in life. A chance to see his fortieth birthday.

Luke picked up a shell and brushed the sand off its rough surface. Then he turned it over and rubbed his finger on the smooth nacre. The soft pastel colors seemed to glow. He cupped the shell in his hand, then sent it skipping out over the water before continuing down the beach.

He shook his head and absently fingered one of his scars. Then he stepped on something hard. He froze, instantly recognizing the distinctive click of an antipersonnel mine. This part of the world was littered with them. The road had been mined, he thought, but the beach should have been safe.

Slowly, he turned his head to search the beach ahead and behind him, but he was the only person on this stretch of sandy coastline.

He closed his eyes and tried to relax. He listened to the roar of the water as another wave rolled toward the beach, then the splashing as the crest broke followed by the sizzle of dissolving sea foam and the sigh of water ebbing back to the sea.

The water had taught him much these last years. No matter that storms might whip it into a frenzy, it always returned to calm. No matter how many tides might rise, an equal number fell. The mightiest aircraft carrier parted the waters on its way from one port to another, but the water always closed in again. Water moved before obstacles, letting them pass with no more notice than a ruffled wake. There was always a cycle, always a return to normalcy.

He considered. Could he look on the ambush as simply a storm whipping his life into a frenzy? Could he look at the success of his career as a rising tide, and Marian's death as its ebb? He opened his eyes and looked out at the blue gulf. Yes, he could see it now. Life was just one big cycle.

"Well, you got what you wanted, Eagle Eye," he said. "Acceptance." He threw back his head and laughed. Then he lifted his foot.

114

Echoes

Dora Archer

Wind tore at Lysander's cloak while flying sand slapped his face with every gust. Two days had gone by since his desperate escape into the desert. His horse had died before the sandstorm only a few hours ago but it seemed like eons. Knowing he would not survive without shelter, he struggled on, despite his body screaming for a few moments of rest. Every breath felt like small daggers piercing his throat, and he kept his eyes cast down in fear of being blinded. Determination to survive drove Lysander on. Survival from the cruel elements of the desert and from the men that forced him to seek escape here.

"Who goes there?"

Lysander raised his head at the call. Bringing his hands up to block some of the sand, he looked about. There was something to his left. He blinked, disbelieving; it seemed to be a fortress. He would have gone by without noticing if not for the call of some guard. The fortress stood strong against the storm, and Lysander felt hope at its promise of shelter. With renewed strength flowing down to his numb limbs, he walked faster. The gates stood open, and Lysander rushed in. The wind didn't howl and pull at him anymore. Inside the walls there was only an eerie stillness. It felt unreal, as if he'd stepped into another world altogether.

Lysander turned towards the gate and saw that it wasn't open; rather it was not there, leaving a gaping mouth in the fortress's wall. He scanned the walls but saw no sentries. Turning to the keep he saw that its doors were also missing. The fortress seemed deserted. Lysander frowned. Someone had called him. "Hellooo! Anyone here?" The wind howling outside was his only answer. Had he imagined that voice? Still, the keep offered shelter until the storm passed.

With a blanket of dust covering everything within the keep, Lysander estimated the place hadn't been used for at least a decade. He tried to remember the region's history. As far as he knew this fortress shouldn't be here. Walking down a long corridor, he came upon a heavy double door made of iron, the only door that still stood. He pushed at it, but the door didn't budge. He tried pushing with his shoulder, and the door swung open slowly with a groan of rusted metal. The room beyond was vast, and Lysander guessed it to be the commander's room if not a noble's.

Lysander grinned; a fitting place for the descendant and namesake of Lysander the Healer. His pursuers wouldn't follow him in the storm—not unless they were foolish or more desperate to catch him that he was to get away.

There was no furniture inside the room but someone had stacked firewood against the wall, next to a fireplace. "Well," Lysander said to the fortress, moving to the fireplace. "Seems like I'm not the only one that sought shelter inside your walls." He picked up a small stick and ran a slender finger over it. A layer of dust transferred to his fingertip. "It seems like it's been a while though."

He pushed the door closed, moved the smaller pieces of wood into the fireplace and coaxed a small fire to life. When he was sure his fire had a good appetite he carefully added bigger fuel to it. Having a decent fire burning cheerfully, Lysander took off his cloak and spread it on the ground. He added more wood to the fire and lay down using his arm as a headrest. He fell asleep watching the flames dance.

•

Lysander sat up and looked around. Something had woken him, but the room was empty and silent, except for his fast breathing. He tried to relax and remember if it was a dream that woke him. Then he heard something outside the door. He held his breath and listened. Footsteps! Lysander slowly stood and backed away from the door, looking around the room for something to use as a weapon. He grabbed a large stick and waited. The footsteps paused right outside the door, silent. Lysander assumed a defensive stance, raised the stick over his head like a sword and almost dropped it when someone pounded loudly on the door three times. Heart racing, Lysander waited; he heard the footsteps again, moving away.

His muscles began to hurt, he didn't know how long he stood there, tense and statue-still, waiting for the intrusion that never came. Whoever the stranger that knocked on the door had been, he had walked away and did not return. Lysander decided to find out what was going on. He was trapped inside this room anyway. Holding the stick in his right hand, ready to strike, Lysander pulled the door open with his left. He looked down the long corridor, but it seemed as deserted as the first time he saw it. Was it a dream? If it was, he hadn't woken up yet, or had he? If it wasn't a dream, why would someone let him know that he knew Lysander was there and then just walk away?

Lysander crept down the corridor and outside, into the fortress's courtyard. The storm no longer howled, but a fog had rolled in. This area never had fog; it was far too dry to be possible. Something moved at the edge of Lysander's vision, and he turned to look upon the wall. A sentry walked its length, his head turned, watching out over the desert.

Swallowing hard Lysander took a few steps forward. "Hello!"

The sentry turned, peered at Lysander and quickly saluted. "What can I do for you, sir?"

Lysander stared, not sure how to answer the question. This wasn't the reaction he expected. "Um, are you the one that called out to me before?"

"No, sir!"

Lysander shifted uncomfortably and, realizing how nervous he must've appeared, stood still again. "Any idea who called me? I'd like to thank him." This was strange.

"No, sir!"

Lysander just stared at the man who still stood at attention, waiting for Lysander's next question. He had none. He probably would have asked many questions if the man hadn't been acting so strangely. Lysander was a stranger here; he had waltzed in and took the commander's quarters and this sentry treated him as if he *was* the commander.

"Permission to speak freely, sir!" the sentry said.

Lysander began shuffling again. "Um, yes, of course, granted."

"Are you feeling well, sir? No offence, sir, but you're not acting like yourself."

Lysander gaped at the man, trying to find a reasonable answer when another sentry appeared seemingly out of nowhere. The newcomer looked down at Lysander and also saluted. "Sir! You better come and look at this."

When Lysander just stood staring at them the sentries glanced at each other. "Sir?" the first one inquired.

"Yes?" Lysander said in a trembling voice.

"Should I call the healer, sir?"

"Um, no, I'm not ill. Um, thank you."

"Sir?" the second sentry said.

"Yes?"

"Will you then come and have a look, sir?"

"Oh, yes! Of course….um how do I get up there?"

The sentries glanced at each other again. "Through the tower, sir," the second sentry finally said. "Over there."

Lysander turned to where the sentry pointed. A tower was built into the wall. "Oh, of course." He looked up at the sentries. "I'll be right there, yes, of course…"

He slowly walked to the tower. Inside a small doorway were stairs leading up. He glanced at the sentries that still stood on the wall looking at him; he entered the doorway and climbed the circular staircase. The sentries waited patiently as Lysander warily approached them.

"Out there, sir," one of them said when Lysander stood in front of them. They were both young, in their early twenties and dressed in plain chain mail. Lysander couldn't tell to whom their loyalty might lay. He looked over the wall out to the desert where the sentry had indicated and saw a glow in the distance.

"Looks like a campfire, sir," the sentry closest to him said. "They must've traveled through that damned storm to be here now."

The sentry's words sent a shiver down Lysander's spine. So, they had followed him through the storm. They really wanted him dead that badly?

"Sir?" the sentry said worriedly. "Are you sure you feel well? You look pale."

"I…um…who's the commander here? To whom are you loyal?" If at least he knew who these men followed, he would have a clue as to whether he would ask for help or not.

The sentries seemed shocked. "You of course, sir!" the first said quickly.

Lysander's jaw all but dropped to the floor. "Me?"

The sentries shifted nervously. "Yes, sir," they both said.

"What are your names?" Lysander asked, not knowing what to answer to that.

"I'm Nern, sir," the first said. "And this is Jaser."

"I'm Lysander."

The worry grew on their faces. "We know who you are, sir," Nern said.

118

"You do?"

"Of course, sir, everyone within these walls knows."

Jaser shifted and smiled. "Is this some kind of test, sir?"

Lysander made a decision then. "Just a bit of fun, gentlemen," he said and grinned, hoping he was doing the right thing and being convincing.

The men laughed. "We heard you had good humor, sir," Jaser said. "But what of the intruders?"

"Oh, yes," Lysander said remembering his pursuers. "Those men are here to assassinate me."

"What!" both men exclaimed. Then Nern asked, uncertain, "Is this another jest, sir?"

"No."

"I'll sound the alarm!" Jaser said and raced to the tower. A moment later a bell rang and the keep came to life.

Soldiers poured out of the keep and gathered in the courtyard so fast Lysander wouldn't have believed it if he hadn't seen it. He was sure the keep had been empty; where did this army come from? A man walked up to the wall and looked at Lysander and the remaining sentry. Jaser still rang the bell. The man below wore an armor that shone silver in the moonlight. This must be the real commander, Lysander thought, his knees suddenly trembling.

The officer turned his head to Lysander and his expression changed from annoyance to something Lysander couldn't interpret. "My Lord!" the man called, and Lysander felt like fainting. "How may we serve you?"

When Lysander didn't speak Nern spoke. "Sir, there are men camped in the field seeking to assassinate Lord Lysander."

This is all madness, Lysander thought, close to hysteria.

"How many?" the soldier below asked.

"I only see one camp, sir."

"For assassins they aren't stealthy then. Send scouts. Maybe they seek to trick us."

"Yes, sir!"

The man turned to Lysander. "Come down, my Lord. We'll handle this."

Lysander nodded and after an uncomfortable silence he learned the captain's name was Darsan.

"Go and see how many there are," Darsan said to the two scouts. "Don't engage, just come back and report."

"Yes, sir!"

Darsan turned to six men standing by the entrance. "Open the gate!"

Lysander was about to ask what gate when the men moved and began pulling at nothing but air. They groaned and pulled as if a gate truly stood there and, when the men had 'pulled' the gate open, the scouts rushed out, and the men began 'pushing' the gates shut.

The process was repeated when the scouts returned. Even though Lysander could see them standing, waiting for the 'gate' to open, he didn't say anything. Everyone acted as if all this was normal so he played the part and hoped for the best.

"Report," said Darsan.

"Only six, sir," the first scout said. "They must be mad. We scouted the forest around them, and they have no other men hidden there. They didn't even place a guard. We could slay them in their sleep."

Well, Lysander thought, of course they didn't place guards. They think they are the ones doing the hunting. How could they imagine I would find an army of insane men that think I'm their commander? And what forest?

Darsan laughed. "If Arel was here he would've made them run all the way back to Lanoria. We can't afford to let them go, however. Take ten men, and kill them."

"Yes, sir!"

Lysander couldn't believe what he had heard. These men though he was *the* Lysander, his great great-great and many more great grandfather! They spoke of Arel as if he had just left this fortress. The legendary shape-shifter that fought next to Lysander the Healer and...Lysander turned to Darsan. "What of Selia the Sorceress?"

"Lady Selia left four years ago, my Lord," Darsan said, looking at Lysander as if he'd grown an extra head. "Arel went with her. The men said you were acting strangely..."

"A little tired is all," Lysander said weakly.

Men were pushing the invisible gates open again, and ten warriors went out. It wasn't long after when the screams began. His would be assassins were screaming as if the hounds of hell were loose upon them. Then suddenly, silence.

120

"I need to lie down," Lysander said to no one in particular and walked as if in a dream back to the commander's room. He didn't know when he fell asleep, but when he woke the keep was silent. The men must've fallen asleep, too, but last night they were cheering their easy victory and making fun of the Lanorians for their feeble attempt to kill their lord. The Lanorians, a people dead and gone for centuries.

He walked out to the corridor and looked around. It once again appeared deserted. How could it manage to look so empty with so many men living here? He strode around the keep, looking for his insane army but found none. The rooms stood empty. He came upon another iron door and pushed it open. The room was empty but painted on the wall was something that made Lysander's blood run cold. There were parts of the painting worn from time, but the faces were clear, one of them was his own…next to him stood Darsan and some of the others he met last night. Below the painting in silver letters it read, 'Lysander and the army of Alesia before the War of Nations.'

Lysander knew of that war. It was the one in which Lysander the Healer fell, along with every soldier under his command. The war Lysander the Healer's allies won, and the nations became one powerful kingdom under the Alesian prince.

Lysander left the keep and ran through the desert to where the men pursuing him had camped. What he saw he never forgot. The bodies appeared drained of blood and their faces beyond the paleness of death; they were as white as snow…but the worst part was the look of horror frozen on their dead faces.

Lysander turned back to look at the keep, but it was gone. Not an army of insane he realized, an army of dead.

FOR LANCELOT

My noble king,
I am but a lowly maiden.
But when you are near
It's like a spell of magic has been cast,
And I find that I am no longer a maiden,
But a queen.

Only you, my king, can perform this art,
For you are a king.
And though the crowds don't flock around
And call praise to your name,
Or hail the beauty of your face,
You are no less a king -
For you are mine.
And in mine eyes I see
No other more noble,
More majestic, or more beautiful than you.
For only in your eyes
Am I a queen.

And just one more thing,
Your majesty, my King.
I love you.

Carrie Chesney

Search & Rescue

Thomas Lynn

Surely there is peace
Beside a soldier's grave

Darkness comes early in a war zone. Soldiers scheduled for a special patrol are more aware of the increasing shadows. Special preparations are taken to blacken faces in order to merge with the night. During this mission, steel helmets are exchanged for the soft pile caps with fur earflaps that are less protective but also quieter and less inclined to slow a guy down. Dog tags are taped together and all insignias removed from uniforms.

Experience teaches that metal has a tendency to bang, clink or clang despite every effort to prevent it. Silence was the rule . . . any deviation could be fatal.

This night's target was Chunjun-ni, a small Korean village near Haeju in the Hwanghae. The patrol was a Wolfpack operation led by Lieutenant Kim Bong Sung. No maps of the area were available during the briefing but Chunjun-ni was too small to show up on a map anyway.

In his briefing, SFC Brad Bergstrom, S3, advised that recent field intelligence suggested several captive American pilots being held in the village pending transfer to a permanent enemy POW camp. One of the unit's primary objectives was the rescue of any allied military forces taken prisoner. The planned raiding party would include two Korean partisan groups with Sgt. Jerry Wheeler and Cpl. Eddie Neal assigned as observers and communicators just in case any American units were encountered. Friendly outposts tended to fire on any group that couldn't speak English.

Bergstrom took Wheeler and Neal aside, cautioning them to be especially alert to the actions and attitude of the partisan officer during this mission. "Lt. Sung is a former North Korean army officer," he explained. "He only recently arrived from Ongjin, and we're not certain yet of his loyalties."

The unit basically consisted of American soldiers with various qualifications to train Koreans from both sides, North and South, to wage guerilla warfare against the North Korean Peoples Army and their Chinese allies. It operated from island bases off the east coast and in the Yellow Sea to launch operational Seek and Destroy as well as Intelligence and Reconnaissance missions in enemy territory against specific strategic targets. Partisans were recruited from the ranks of former river pirates and army defectors who volunteered to fight against the communist invaders for their own reasons, whether political or personal.

"Hey, Sarge! Ain't it kinda risky sending this guy out so early?" Wheeler echoed Neal's thoughts.

"That's why we're sending you two along—to keep an eye on him." As Operations NCO, Bergstrom practically called the shots on guerilla missions. "Lt. Sung came here with a group of North Korean dissidents to link up with us, and he comes highly recommended by Leopard." He referred to a sister partisan unit north of Wolfpack sector. North Korea also used partisans to infiltrate and to cause sabotage in the south. This officer could possibly be an enemy mole.

The two Americans anxiously prepared their weapons and thermal clothing for what might lie ahead. They taped two ammo magazines together so they could be reversed quickly for reloading. Each magazine carried thirty rounds, but Wheeler and Neal drew extra ammo, thereby providing them with more than 200 rounds of firepower each.

"All this for observers?" Neal wondered aloud for it seemed a lot. "Just how much observing is really expected from the two of us?" They test-fired their weapons against the side of a hill and then from supply drew individual PRC/10 radio transceivers wrapped in special black waterproofed canvas cases. Neither noted anything remarkable or unusual about Lt. Kim Bong Sung as they were introduced, except that he was a big man, well over six feet in height, muscular, with the usual impassive facial expression. A quick glance at the partisans assigned to participate in the mission showed uniforms and equipment similar in appearance. American infantry patrols usually consisted of at least one Thompson submachine gun or a BAR but partisan patrols were armed only with M2 Carbines, which could be fired in single rounds or on full automatic depending on the situation. Wheeler and Neal also carried .45s, as did the patrol leader. Everyone assigned to this operation was dressed to get in and get out quickly. It was obvious that these guys had done this before.

In the murky obscurity of night, the raiding party assembled and boarded two fishing junks for passage north from Kanghwa, hugging the island's coastline until passing between Kyodong-do and Songmo. The boats then headed due west toward open water, keeping the North Korean shoreline on their starboard side. Despite all precautions, the icy fingers of winter quickly found their way inside Neal's parka. He shifted the weight of his weapon slightly for a more comfortable fit while his ears felt the frosty air, and his toes grew numb inside two pairs of socks. On the trailing junk he and Wheeler huddled over the dubious warmth of a hibachi in the forward cabin while Lt. Sung commanded the other vessel. Maybe one of them should have accompanied the lieutenant but there was no real reason for it. Besides, neither was conversationally fluent in the Korean language.

Hours passed as the indistinct shoreline glided by unconcerned about the presence of the two vessels. The moon hung low in the sky, and a thin misty vapor hovered over the water to paint everything in a ghostly reflection. Soon the engines ceased without warning, and they drifted between wind and tide in the waters of the Yellow Sea, far from friendly faces. The two Americans cupped their hands, smoked cigarettes and in soft whispers learned a little about each other.

Wheeler was a former paratrooper with the 187th Airborne RCT. He had been wounded in both legs at Wonsan and airlifted home for medical treatment. When his wounds healed, he requested another combat tour.

"Why, Jerry?"

"You mean, why did I come back?"

"Yeah."

"I don't know. I guess because the folks back home didn't seem to care or understand what was happening here. They kept asking why we let these gooks push us around. Why didn't we mop up on them like in World War II? I couldn't explain to them that the Chinese and North Koreans weren't only excellent soldiers, but they outnumbered and outgunned us as well. Maybe I just got tired of everybody's indifferent attitude toward this war."

"Why didn't you go back to the 187th?"

"They didn't think my legs could handle any more jumps. I didn't really care."

"So you wound up in this outfit." Wheeler was candid in reply. "I heard about the special partisan forces and went to see Colonel Lowry. He didn't have to pull many strings to have me assigned to this unit. So here I am." The two of them talked and watched the shadowy antics of darkness cavorting around them, awaiting the signal to get underway again. Luminescent waves slapped against the wooden hulls, but the moonlight reflected only slightly from the surrounding water. Cigarettes were shared, and they guardedly smoked, biding time as best they could. High tide was due at 0330, and although the junks were not deep draft vessels, they still required as much leeway as possible to clear the shoals and shallow bottoms at the harbor entrance. Tides varied between 20 and 40 feet, which meant the patrol group had only a few hours to complete its mission before returning to the safety of the channel.

Neither flash of light nor low thunder of distant guns gave any indication of war's presence as they rode the gentle swells of that sea. Lost in thought, Neal was startled when both engines abruptly broke the silence. He felt the forward motion as his boat immediately lurched ahead, certain that the enemy would hear the sound of their approach. Wheeler smiled and put his forefinger and thumb together in the universal "OK" sign. His companion wished he was as confident.

Thin streaks of gray overhead announced the birth of another frigid dawn as the flotilla entered the bay of Haeju and the echo of engines again died in unison. From that point the boats proceeded slowly and silently by means of oarsmen seated at the stern, propelling them with a "wiggle-stick," a sort of oar moving rapidly back and forth in the water to provide a forward motion. It was a method of thrust unique to oriental boatmen.

An icy wind blew steadily as they rode the tide into Haeju Bay like pirates stalking a worthy target, slipping past unknown silhouettes eerily revealed in the wintry somber gloom. Scanning the shoreline they searched for flickering lights. Unbelievably, no movement was evidenced at the landing site and no audible alarms betrayed them. Eddie Neal marveled at actually landing two full boatloads of armed soldiers in a hostile land without being observed.

The darkness had gratefully embraced them for the moon slept and spectral mists disguised the raider's wake. The boats were opaque silhouettes gliding onward until forward motion finally ceased altogether. The soldiers braced themselves as their boat gently slapped the side of a jutting pier and within seconds everyone scrambled ashore to converge among the shadows.

Lieutenant Sung motioned Neal over to him and whispered, "Corporal-san, you stay close. We move quick now." So saying, he raised his arm and gestured his men to move out. They were now two separate patrols — Jerry in one, Neal in the other. Without further word, the patrols moved forward. Neal glanced over his shoulder to see the ghostly junks abandoning them, absconding on receding waves.

Patches of ice and crusty snow blanketed the ground and Neal soon forgot about the intense cold. He remained one step behind as the lieutenant swiftly inspected the area for enemy signs. A quick assessment led Neal to the conclusion that this officer was typically arrogant like most Orientals appeared to be in a leadership position. Lt. Sung held his chin high, and his eyes were thin slits gazing long at one place before moving on. Apparently satisfied they were not detected, he began a jaunty stride across uneven terrain and maintained the same pace for more than a mile. At one point he slowed somewhat but still kept moving at a hard march only to resume a double-time gait.

The swinging motion of the radio chafed Neal's shoulder. His legs ached with every step. The steady pace soon had him panting like a tired race horse, and he fervently wished Lt. Kim Bong Sung would fall and break a leg just so they could stop and rest. He stole a glance at the others, noting how they too were experiencing difficulty keeping up. It made him feel less like the physically weak American soldier that he knew he was.

Wheeler and the other patrol came to mind. Where were they? Were the two separate groups supposed to converge on Chunjun-ni from different directions? It occurred to Neal that they could mistakenly fire upon each other. Such things happened during battle. He recalled the prime example of General Custer dividing his troops at the Little Big Horn. This part of the operation wasn't mentioned during the briefing back at Wolfpack Base, but he wasn't as upset about that as about not intuitively knowing more about this kind of thing. Berating himself for being such a green recruit kept his mind occupied, and his legs continuing to plough ahead during the torturous grind.

Forward progress slowed when the patrol avoided the rutted road in favor of the less imposing rolling hills dotted with a few bare shrubs. Neal almost cried with joy when the lieutenant signaled for a halt upon reaching a rocky rise. He had fallen back, but now he moved up beside the patrol leader. The pain in his shoulders and legs began to subside as he gazed at a gently declining slope in front of them, bordered on two sides by steep hills without any noticeable protective cover. Between the hills a narrow rivulet appeared, and then the target village lodged precariously on the near side of a bend in the near-frozen stream. It was now full daylight, and the lack of movement caused the biting cold to once more creep within Neal's clothing. He knelt beside the lieutenant and studied the North Korean village less than 300 yards away.

"Corporal-san, please to tell other patrol our location." With a nod, Neal raised the transmitter to his lips.

"Lobo One, Lobo One. This is Lobo Two. Over."

"Lobo Two from Lobo One, Over."

"Lobo One from Lobo Two. We have reached target area. Over."

"Lobo Two. This is Lobo One. Roger. Out."

He asked the officer where the other patrol was and learned that it remained behind to secure the landing area for their return.

Okay. At least he discovered that much.

The deep snow appeared unbroken by any natural barriers ahead, offering no visible cover from their ridge position to the village. How were they going to pull this one off without being seen or raked by concealed enemy machinegun fire? Neal had seen too many war movies in which an attacking patrol was ambushed by defenders under similar circumstances. Again, Custer at the Little Bighorn came to mind. He could almost hear the regimental song *Garry Owen* signaling the whisper of death surrounding the Seventh Cavalry regiment.

The unmistakable odor of kimchi permeated the air even at this distance. Lt. Sung motioned the patrol ahead, across the crisp snow underfoot. Everybody spread out at regular intervals, and the unmistakable voice of John Wayne suddenly sounded clear and very near.

"All right men!" Neal imagined. "This is it. Let's move out." Obediently, Neal held his rifle in front of him, finger on the trigger, and started down the hill with a growl building in his throat.

The Duke would have been proud.

They moved rapidly toward the village, and he was still alarmed about being sucked into a trap. He was also fearful of tripping over roots or rocks hidden under the snow, but their advance brought them into the open settlement. The patrol swiftly fanned out to secure the perimeter while other troops scurried into the nearest houses.

Much shouting and shoving followed as the Korean partisans herded the residents roughly into the cold wintry air while other houses and buildings were searched. The hardened proficiency of these guerillas was impressive but Neal quietly wanted to know, *where were the captive American airmen?*

There was no trace of the downed pilots. Questioning of the villagers elicited only the information they had been moved the day before to an unknown area. "So much for our vaunted intelligence network," Neal muttered.

Their mission appeared to be unfruitful until a commotion originated from one of the native houses. Something was happening! He hurried over and entered the crude one-room hut. Inside were four NKPA soldiers seated with their backs against the dried mud wall, their hands tied behind their backs and staring at the barrels of five menacing rifles. Fresh blood flowed down the cheek of one of them and he exhibited great astonishment to see an American soldier facing him.

With nervous hand gestures and in unfamiliar English he looked at Neal and asked, ". . . merican! Kill . . . us?"

Neal shook his head, and the prisoner chattered to his companions. Some of the fear went out of their eyes until Lt. Sung and the one who had spoken exchanged a torrent of words, after which the officer lashed out and slapped each of the prisoners hard. Their hands were then roughly tied behind their backs, and they were forced outside.

Lt. Sung seemed obligated to explain. "Corporal-san," he waved his hands at the four North Koreans. "They run from battle. Hide here."

Why should he be so uptight? Hadn't he deserted from the same army? Neal asked the lieutenant if he intended to question them about the missing American pilots.

"No talk," he replied. "Americans all samo samo gone to other place."

"Well, I think we should take them back to Kanghwa for interrogation." The lieutenant's face was unreadable. "No take prisoner."

"What do you plan to do with them?"

"No take prisoner!" he repeated in a rising voice. Plainly he had no intention of releasing them unharmed, and Neal certainly wanted no part of any execution. He decided to push the issue.

"Lieutenant, we have to deliver these prisoners to S-2. They're the only ones who might know what happened to the American pilots. They *must* return with us for questioning."

A hint of annoyance flashed in the officer's eyes as he quickly turned to face the brash young American. For a long undecided moment the two stared at each other. Neal admittedly felt intimidated by the other's eyes. Then he watched the officer's hand begin to move imperceptibly toward the Colt .45 pistol at his side. The other members of the patrol stood silently observing the confrontation. This man could kill him easily without the slightest disturbance of his conscience and without any interference from anyone in the patrol. Neal felt he may have gone too far but he couldn't back down. It was essential that Wolfpack intelligence personnel have the opportunity to interrogate these prisoners. He insisted on this but the lieutenant's hand continued to move threateningly toward his sidearm. His eyes narrowed even more but Neal thought he was bluffing. His only recourse was to push him harder.

He raised the PRC/10 quickly and pressed the push-to-talk button.

"Lobo One. This is Lobo Two, Over."

The tension in his voice must have been evident because the reply came immediately.

"Lobo Two from Lobo One. Send your message. Over."

"Stand by!" He kept the transmitter button depressed and stared at Lt. Sung. Would he pull his weapon and blow the American away? It was a good possibility but if he did, the action would be caught by the open microphone and transmitted instantly to Wheeler in the other patrol. Neal held his breath for what seemed a long wait. He could almost hear the wheels turning in the lieutenant's head. At last he nodded and turned away. Everyone in the room seemed to relax at the same time. Neal's voice was shaky as he completed the radio transmission. "Lobo One. This is Lobo Two. We are departing this area with four prisoners. Over."

"Lobo Two from Lobo One. Roger, Understood. Out."

But he and the lieutenant weren't through yet.

"One more thing, Lieutenant Sung. We'll need warm clothing for the prisoners." Neal held his breath but the officer gave the command without hesitation.

Chunjun-ni faded behind them as the patrol retraced its steps up the ridge and across the snow-covered hills toward the boat landing area. Perhaps to demonstrate that he was still the leader of this patrol, Lt. Sung continued the same brutal pace as before with no regard for the four prisoners struggling to keep up.

Neal thought he had a pretty good line on this former North Korean officer after their little confrontation. But he was yet to learn that above everything else, the man *was* a soldier!

The afternoon was growing late and a light snow began to fall. Footing was difficult as they kept off the road and tried to step in their previous footpaths to avoid the unseen drifts. At one point they paused briefly to rest and Neal felt no sensation in his feet at all. He thought the landing area was just over the next rise but he couldn't be sure since he'd lost all track of time. It was important to return to the boats quickly because the tide wouldn't wait. They started to move out when they were suddenly rocked by two quick explosions.

Grenades!

Two partisans went down at once, the snow stained with the rush of their blood. One of them yelled and threw up his hands in a protective motion. He twisted as he fell and died from the force of the blast. The other man was lifted off his feet where he now lay crumpled in the snow. Neal unslung his rifle and dove at the nearest white mound for cover as the rattle of a Chinese burp gun pinned them down. When he raised his head to check on the prisoners, the lieutenant yelled at him. The words were unintelligible but Neal surmised that he was telling him to keep his stupid American head down. Meanwhile, the patrol had dispersed and was returning fire, but it was doubtful any of them saw a verifiable target.

Neal still didn't know what was happening and every time he attempted to rise up to take a look, the lieutenant yelled at him. In anger Neal rolled away and found himself in a shallow depression that afforded some protection and a field of vision. From this location he identified several Chinese soldiers in their peculiar quilted uniforms, kneeling in an open area and shooting. Didn't they know enough to hide behind a tree or rock? He switched his carbine on full automatic and fired two long bursts without stopping. Trying hastily to reverse the clip to fire again, he dropped it in the snow. Panic gripped him as he fumbled around for it, knowing that the enemy was out there shooting at him. Necessity forced him to remove a glove to locate clip and wipe away the snow before inserting it into his weapon.

Lt. Sung, meanwhile, crawled to a point where he could direct a crossfire. His quick vocal commands and immediate response of his men turned the situation around. The patrol took the offense, hitting the attackers from several directions. Neal wondered why no more grenades were tossed in their direction.

The sound of bullets in old western movies had a peculiar whine as they sailed harmlessly overhead but Neal heard real bullets, whirring softly like angry hornets. He was busy alternately shooting and ducking and didn't immediately hear the crackle of his radio.

At length, Neal recognized Wheeler's voice. "Lobo Two from Lobo One." Wheeler must have heard the gunfire as his voice was excited. "What's your situation? Over."

"This is Lobo Two. We're under fire at a point northeast of your location. Over."

"Roger. We're on the way. Lobo One Out."

When Lt. Sung glanced at him; Neal lifted his fist with the thumb raised and hoped Koreans understood that gesture. Apparently they did and the lieutenant turned back to the business at hand. Lt. Sung was all over the area, firing as he ran from one position to another, directing the members of his patrol. Neal had to admit he was a good combat leader. Neal stole a quick peek from behind his cover in time to see two Chinese soldiers jump up and start to run directly toward his position. Reflexes took over as he brought his weapon to bear and squeezed off a continuous burst while traversing left to right. The two Chinese soldiers went down hard, their weapons flying through the air and their bodies kicking in the snow. Even as he watched them fall, Neal's finger refused to ease up on the trigger until the entire clip was empty. A frenzy of rifle fire followed a muffled shout as Wheeler's group joined the action.

The enemy patrol had committed a tactical error launching their attack without sufficient defensive cover. Ignorance of the second patrol's existence left the Chinese caught in an inescapable vise. They continued to fight, but Neal watched them drop one by one on that hill until none remained alive.

Neal watched the men in the patrol walk among those prone bodies, and single shots echoed at various intervals until all was silent. As each shot rang out, Lt. Sung stared blankly at Neal as if seeking a reaction. Neal, however, turned his back and walked away. After all, a *coup de grace* wasn't purely an Oriental art.

The patrol lost two of its prisoners and six of their own members. Time to board the fishing junks once again. Wheeler and Neal were delighted to hear the engines rev up as the junks churned out toward deep water. Even though there was no intelligence developed concerning the captive American fighter pilots, the mission did result in two enemy prisoners. Perhaps interrogation would be able to locate them after all and another mission scheduled.

For some reason, the temperature seemed less frigid on the return trip.

Finding the Calm

Faceless automatons
Right-foot-stepping out the commuter train door
In endless crowds of
Unseeing eyes.

Join the mob,

Seeking one face.

Searching dark dreams
Filled with shadow
And half-shadow
And shades of gray.

Running in and out,

Seeking light.

Casting about,
Hurried and harried,
Edging toward panic
As time slips away.

And then I find

You.

Cynthia Bateman

The Simplicity of It

Jamie Lin

"Baby, I can give you the world," he said when he proposed that spring. It was the most romantic thing that had ever come out of his mouth. She said yes and gave up everything else for their life together.

Looking around the apartment three years later, she wanted to cry. The ceiling leaked from last night's rain. Roaches crawled around the rust in the bathroom while water dripped. Ashes added a new layer to the coffee table while empty beer cans cluttered every corner of the room, and no matter how many times a week she cleaned, they'd always be back, constantly reminding her of their lifestyle. Whenever either of them felt stressed, they would reach for stimulants.

She came home one morning at 5:13 with a migraine and abdominal cramps. Collapsing on the bed with helplessness in her eyes, she thought about going to see a doctor. But the cookie jar had been empty since last Tuesday, and her legs felt like they were made of stones. The doctor would tell her the same thing as last time anyway, that she worked too hard and didn't sleep enough. Waking up a few hours later with sunlight glaring in her face, she smelled blood and felt a warm wetness between her legs. She glanced down and threw up in her mouth.

When he came home that night, he found her in the bathtub with blood stains on the cracked tiles. He asked what happened, almost irritated at the mess in front of him. She explained in a dull voice that made his heart beat a little faster.

"Honey, I'm so sorry." He pulled her head into his lap and held her. "We'll try again."

She nodded with puffy, unblinking eyes. Her expression, one of utter emptiness and loss, caused his throat to become clogged with uneasiness. He took care of her for the next few days, first by moving anything baby-related to the closet. And each night, once he got home, he'd take the time to make dinner from an ancient cookbook he'd found somewhere. Before going to sleep, he would try to make her smile and laugh by bringing home movies and comics. Things returned to normal, eventually. She bought a new pair of shoes and went back to work.

The apartment started to smell like cigarettes again. Within a few weeks, beer cans flooded the living room and kitchen again. She asked him what was wrong one evening after discovering that he never got out of bed. "I got fired," he said, eyes never leaving the television. He took another drag from his cigarette. "I didn't do anything wrong, babe. The boss was whack."

Her shoulders immediately dropped, giving her the appearance of being twice her age. Her head felt ready to burst with all the conflicts in her mind. How was she going to support the two of them? But she carried on, sleeping a little less and working a little more, trying to remain sane and in control.

One rowdy night at the diner a few weeks later, she suddenly felt her stomach swirl like a merry-go-round. "Hey, miss! I wanted ice in this!" someone screamed. Three other people yelled out something too, but she didn't hear. Rushing to the bathroom in the back, she faced the yellow toilet and vomited her grilled cheese and fries. Within seconds she knew what was happening. She'd been through this before. Julia told her boss she was ill and walked out despite his outraged protests. The cold night air whipped about her face like sharp needles, but she found it refreshing compared to the stuffiness inside with all the yelling, crying and laughing.

She went home after an hour to a grouchy husband who had been wearing the same "Vote for Pedro" T-shirt and green shorts for the past two weeks. She studied his face and wondered when it had become a chore to love him. Before, she had felt like they were the only two in the world, surrounded by nothing but love and dreams. Now she couldn't help but mentally list all of his flaws and weaknesses every time she saw him. She wondered when the magic flew out of their relationship. She still cared, but it was different. Every time he opened his mouth, she would feel her shoulders twitch. She couldn't go on like this; all these bills. He kept getting fired every two or three months. They would never have a stable income or life. And she knew better than to ask him to change. He was who he was, and that was why she loved him. She thought about the past, and by the time the sun climbed upward toward the top of the sky, she knew what she had to do.

She kissed him goodbye when he told her he was going to a buddy's. "Here. Take a twenty." She stuffed it into his shirt pocket. "Have fun."

"Thanks!" He kissed her twice more on the lips with a big childish grin.

She smiled back and genuinely wished him well. Sitting down at the kitchen table, she wrote a letter--brief, straightforward, well wished, and ending with "All my love, Julia." She took the train with her light suitcase. Her knees wouldn't stop shaking for the entire four-hour ride. She prepared a speech, beginning and ending with an apology, including a couple in the middle too. But the moment the door opened and she saw her parents' faces, she couldn't do anything but break down and cry. It was the first time her parents had seen her in over three years; the first time Julia's mother ever embraced and kissed her, mixing their salty tears together. Her mind suddenly cleared, and she felt solid ground under her feet once again.

The baby weighed seven pounds and three ounces. Julia named her second child — Chance.

Eros at My Window

Warm, awake morning;
Glassy window boomed, as in a knock.
I thought Eros was at my window
Again.

I rose to find an empty sky plagued with wind
Faceless, moving everything.

Dare not to tame Eros.

He was invisible to me,
Yet his movement still I see
Bend each branch in fickle harmony...

Dare not to tame Eros.

And valentines become his spells
Chanted in charming tongues,
Fairies ever strange to me,
Curling locks and satyr's songs,

And all the nymphs and all the gods
Waver before my eyes
As shadows poisoned
By this strange, quick passing fertile death.

If 'tis Eros at my window
'tis a restless wind indeed.

Robin Layne

BETRAYAL

Carrie Chesney

February 28, 2004

She lay against his chest, panting and sweating. He tightened his arms around her and held her close. Johnica was a great wife, and a great mother, but she was a spectacular lover. She clamped her mouth onto his, showing him that even when it was over, it was never over. He smiled, kissing her neck and trailing his index fingers delicately up either side of her body with a butterfly light touch. She giggled at the sensations it sent through her.

"I love you, John, my favourite wife."

"I'd better be your only wife, Dr. Hopkins."

"Hmm. Let me think about that for a minute," he teased. Her nails raked down his back threateningly. "Okay, I've thought about it. I can't remember any others, so I guess you're the only one. Why would I want anyone else when I have you, sweetheart? You're the only one who excites me." He let his fingers roam through her light brown hair and stroke her cheeks. "You're my everything, Johnica. I'd be so lost and empty without you."

"Joel, can't you stay with me a bit longer? I need more time with you. We never seem to have any cuddling time afterwards. We hardly get any spontaneous time any more, either. Between all your hours at the hospital and the kids, everything is always so planned. I know I shouldn't complain, honey, because when we do get time together, you're so totally awesome. I just need more time with you, more spontaneity, more you at home." She couldn't hold her tears back, and they slid silently down. "I need you, Joel. Please." He had no idea how truly lonely she was. He'd promised her that when the residency was finished and he was in practice, he'd have more time. Five years later things still hadn't worked that way, and it seemed he had less time than before. She loved the kids, but she felt like a single parent.

"I'm sorry, Johnica. I know it isn't the way we want it. In a few years the kids will be older, and we won't have to worry about middle of the night feedings, or little people with nightmares wanting to climb in with us. We'll have a lot more private time then, honey."

"I know. It'll get better. I guess all couples go through this stage. The kids can sit in front of a television mesmerized for hours at a time, but as soon as we try to sneak a little time for us, it's like radar with them. Suddenly they need all the attention, and they usually bang on the door right at the worst possible moment, frustrating the time we do have. I just feel like I'm always waiting. Waiting to finish school, waiting to finish your residency, waiting for the practice to get established, now waiting for the kids to get older."

"I love you more than the day I married you Johnny, and that day I thought I was gonna burst with it. Honey, I have something to tell you. I was going to take you out for dinner to break the news, but I think I should tell you now. I had a meeting with my associates this morning." He moved to lay beside her, and she curled up against his side. "We're changing the way things are scheduled at the office and hospital, so I'll be home a lot more often. You'll probably get sick of seeing me, I'll be here so much. I promised it, and now I can manage it. You're not the only one who's been missing and needing. Things'll be a lot better from now on." He knew it was hard for her, being home with three small children. It left her less and less time to spend with her friends, but over the years she had almost never complained. It was only at times like this, when the love making left her feeling vulnerable, that she asked for more from him.

Really, Joel? I can count on you being here?" She looked at him with hope and fear that it wouldn't come true.

"Absolutely. I never expected you to raise these kids on your own. Three days left of this craziness. I'm determined to keep the promises I made you all those years ago. I'm sorry it took so long, but we're here now, Honey."

"Thank you, Joel. This means so much. It's gonna change everything for me, starting today." She held him tightly. "I can't begin to tell you what a gift this is. I love you. I'll always love you, Joel. No one but you. I never have, and I never will." She clung to him while relief flooded through her, body and soul. He'd never know just how badly she needed this from him.

"We'll always be together, honey, don't worry. Nothing in this world could tear me from you. Now, want to take a shower with me while we can? Sounds like Becca's still sleeping."

"I suppose," she grinned. Life couldn't possibly get any better than this.

Joel thought the sun rose and set on his wife. They had fallen in love when they were eighteen. Together they had learned the wonders of making love, both secure in the knowledge there had never been anyone else in their lives or in their beds. Fourteen years later, they were still as happy and as hungry for one another as they'd been in those early days.

Johnica stepped into the shower with him and washed his shoulders and his stomach. Scooting around to get behind him, she wrapped her arms around his waist and laid her head on his back. She wanted to be the center of his world, like he was for her. Joel shut the water off. They got out, towelled each other dry, smiling all the while. Going into their dressing room, he redressed, putting on a clean shirt and Johnica put her jeans and sweater back on. One of her favourite things was to sit with her legs curled up, watching him get dressed. She loved every step along the way. Doing up the buttons on his shirt, the flips of the tie, even putting on socks. It all made her happy.

The baby started crying. Johnica went to the nursery and picked her up, carrying her on a hip. Joel dropped an arm around her shoulders, and dropped a kiss on the baby as she walked him to the front door. Passing the family room, he stopped to say goodbye to the other kids. "Drayden, Sammy, Daddy's going back to work now. Can I have a kiss before I go?"

Drayden, at three and half, was too involved in his Arthur cartoon to be bothered, but Samantha ran to her daddy. She wrapped her five year old arms around his neck and planted a very wet kiss on his mouth. "I love you, Daddy."

"I love you too, Sammy. You be good for Mommy. Help her out if she needs it, okay?"

"Yes, Daddy. Do I have to be nice to Drayden though? He gets so annoying sometimes."

"I know it can be tough, but remember, he's littler than you. He's not supposed to be as smart as you yet. Play nicely, and this weekend we'll go out for a Daddy-daughter date. Wherever you want to go."

"Okay, Daddy. I'll think of something very special." She kissed him again and then wiggled until he put her down, and she went back to sit with Drayden, instantly hypnotised by the tube.

With a final goodbye kiss for his wife, he was out the door and on his way to bring some more babies into the world. Johnica went to the kitchen where her day carried on, rubbing Ora-gel on the gums of a teething baby, answering phone calls regarding play dates and dropping it all to go fix the toilet, again. Another day in domestic paradise, and she was happy with her life.

Late in the afternoon, the two little ones were in the backyard playing in the snow, and the baby was ready for sleep. Johnica retrieved her journal, wanting to write about the news her husband had given her.

February 27, 2004
This has been one of the best days of my entire life. I have everything I've ever wanted and more. Joel has worked so hard, putting in so many extra hours because he insisted I have a big house, an expensive car, expensive clothes, the best of everything. I know he did those things because he loves me, but I would have done without all of it, if it meant having more time with him. That's all I've ever wanted. To be with him and enjoy our family together.

Today he came home at lunch, right after Becca fell asleep, and we went to bed. Today he told me my dream is finally coming true. He's going to become a full time husband and parent, not just someone who drops in when he can. I thought this day would never come.

As I'm sitting here nursing Becca, I suddenly seem to love her even more. My love for Joel spills out into my love for our children. I want to plan something special for when I tell him our good news. I know he'll be so excited. He always is.

I called D. a short time ago and broke the news. We're going to meet tonight. D. doesn't sound happy that it's going to be over between us. I was almost afraid when we spoke. I'll be glad it's over. I just wish I'd never told the truth. I think that's what's going to cause problems. My biggest regret, as this path comes to an end, is that I ever took it. I wish I was a stronger person, strong enough to be what Joel wants me to be.

I have three beautiful children that I love more than life, and the greatest husband in the world. I love Joel above all else. My life is perfect with him at my side. In spite of my mistakes, I am so blessed. Thank you God.

J. L. H.

•

He picked up the phone and dialled 911. With an attempt to disguise his voice, he reported a fire at the Sage Motor Inn. The motel was a few miles outside of town. It would take time for the trucks to respond. After hanging up, he lit matches and dropped them on the body one by one.

She was awake, but unable to move, unable to make a sound. Her eyes reflected the horror her spirit endured, the pain her body was suffering. She never dreamed that the man she had gone to for physical comfort these past few years could be such a demon. Her eyes searched his, begging for her life. It was no use. His course of action was set from the moment he dropped the rohypnol into her wine glass.

He reasoned that she brought this all on herself. She never should have tried to end things like this. Not with everything they had been through the past few years.

The fire spread quickly, and it was only moments before the entire bed was engulfed in flames. Walking calmly, he left the room and got in his car, driving away. He didn't even look back at the tragedy he'd left behind.

The ambulance parked behind the fire trucks outside a motel on Highway 287, west of Sweetwater Station. It looked to be confined to one unit, but looks could be deceptive. The manager informed them that he thought the room was rented.

Paramedics Tara Shepherd and Justin Cassidy arrived on the scene moments after the fire in room 15 had been extinguished. They had the gurney out, ready to transport. One of the firemen went inside, searching for occupants. He found a body lying on the bed burned beyond recognition but miraculously still alive—barely. Lifting as carefully, yet as quickly as he could, he carried it to the paramedics.

Tara was aghast. She'd seen pictures of badly burned bodies before, but this was no picture. She moved swiftly, covering the body with a clean sterile sheet and gently securing it. Tara climbed into the back of the ambulance with her patient. Justin locked the back doors and climbed into the cab of the vehicle. He pulled back onto the highway, lights flashing and siren blasting, not that there was anybody else on the road. After all, this was a Wednesday night in Wyoming.

Lander Valley Medical Centre was their destination. Tara's father, Dr. Matt Shepherd was on duty when they arrived. He noticed some of the nurses cringing uncontrollably from the stench of the burnt flesh. It was a smell you never forgot.

"Because of all the damage, I was afraid to intubate in the van, so I just bagged him/her, " Tara told him.

Looking at the body, Matt wasn't able to immediately determine whether his patient was male or female either. When the body had been transferred to the examining table in the trauma room Matt began his assessments. With great care he intubated the patient and connected the oxygen. He followed the rule of nines in assessing the extent of the burns. The flesh no longer had an epidermis or a dermis level left. Some areas were charred through the subcutaneous tissue to the bone. He wasn't sure why the heart was still pumping. It shouldn't be. The body was 73% covered with fourth degree burns. It took a lot of searching to find a place where there was enough skin to insert an IV of saline with electrolytes to try to rehydrate the body, what there was of it. A nurse finally inserted it on the bottom of the right foot.

Matt was depressed by the amount of debriding that would be necessary if the patient lived. The removal of all the charred, dead tissue. He needed a specialist in plastics for a consult, but Lander didn't have one. Even if he sent for one to be flown in, he doubted the patient would survive long enough. He hated taking such a pessimistic view, but he couldn't help seeing the situation for what it really was. Hopeless.

"Meghan, draw some blood for the lab. We don't have time to wait for them to send someone down. I want them to run the complete gambit on it. It doesn't make sense that someone would allow themselves to be this badly burned without making an effort to get out, unless there were drugs or alcohol inhibiting movement, which would also explain why he didn't die from smoke inhalation. Check the body for any jewellery. It needs to be removed before edema starts.

"Sarah, I want a sterile sheet to cover the body with. We're going to douse it with cold water and let it soak for five minutes. After that we'll need dry sterile sheets to cover the body. Damn, what we really need is a hyper baric chamber." He listened to the chest to see if both sides were making equal breathing sounds. At least it was still inflating.

By the time he was done, Sarah was covering the body and had a number of buckets filled with cold water to be poured on. She had also arranged for someone from housekeeping to be there to keep the floor relatively dry using the floor squeegee as they worked.

"Dad."

"Yes Meg."

"Dad, can I speak to you privately for a minute?"

"Not now, Meghan."

"This is important."

Irritated by his daughter's insistence, he pulled away from his work. "Sarah, you're all right carrying on with watering down the body? Make sure it goes onto the sheet, not directly onto the skin."

"Yes, Dr. Shepherd."

Matt turned away from the patient and stepped closer to the trauma room door. "I can't believe you'd ask to speak to me privately at a time like this, Meghan. This patient is critical, so you'd better have …"

"I know who she is, Dad," she interrupted. "There's engraving in the wedding ring."

Matt looked at the inner circle of the ring and felt as though he'd been punched in the solar plexis. "Oh, God, no," he exclaimed, his voice barely above a whisper. He closed his eyes to regain his equilibrium. When he felt solid again, he gave orders. "Get Dominic Dante on the phone. Tell him I need him here stat, that he needs to see me directly when he arrives."

"Yes, sir." Meghan closed her fingers over the rings in her hand as she went to place the call. It was hard to stay removed and calm in the face of tragedy when you knew the patient so well.

Ten minutes later, Meghan let Dr. Sheppard know that Dr. Dante had arrived. Matt left his patient and went to see him.

"Dom, thanks for coming. Let's step into the doctor's lounge." He moved to the door and went in, holding it for Dominic to follow after him. "Let's sit." He settled on the edge of the sofa while Dominic sat in a yellow covered chair situated perpendicular to the couch.

"You don't look so good. What's wrong, Matt?" Dominic asked. He'd sent his date home early when he got the call, and she'd been none to pleased about it. Seeing Matt's face, he was glad he'd taken the call.

"We've had a patient come in. Chances of survival are nil. Dominic, it's Johnica Hopkins. I'm sorry, we can't save her."

Dominic felt as though the world had just spun off it's axis. This was the last thing he'd expected to hear when he'd gotten the call. His brain instantly scrambled and he tried to think through it. What was he supposed to ask? "What?!! What happened to her? Does Joel know?"

"Three-quarters of her body has fourth degree burns. I can't tell you much of the circumstances. She came in on the ambulance. We identified her by her wedding ring. I haven't told Joel yet. That's why I asked you to come. He's gonna need a friend tonight."

Dominic started to cry. "Not Johnica. They've got three kids, heck, one's still nursing. Those kids need their mother. Joel needs her. This is so wrong, Matt. So wrong. She's one of the best people I know. Everyone loves Johnny." He swiped quickly at the misting in his eyes and grabbed a tissue to blow his nose. "Can I see her before we bring him down here? He's on call in maternity tonight."

"Certainly, Dom. Go ahead."

Dominic struggled to get enough control to stand, burying his face in his hands. He'd known Johnica forever. He'd gone to med school with Joel and met her soon after they had started dating. He was a fixture in their home. He was Uncle Nicky to their kids. He loved Johnny like a sister. He couldn't believe this was happening. Not to her. Not now. They'd decided just this morning to set up a new system so Joel could be home with her more.

After the initial shock began to wear off the urgency of the situation hit him, and he managed to slowly lift himself from the chair. Matt reached out a steadying hand and walked with him into the trauma room.

Shocked to see her lying there, without a face, he didn't know what to think. Did it make it less real that it was her? He moved to her side wanting to take her hand, but there was nothing to hold onto. The skin was charred to the bone. Part of the fingers were missing. He leaned to where her ear had been. "Johnny, it's Nicky. I'm here, John. I'm bringing Joel to be with you. You hang on, honey. He'll be here in just a minute. I love you, Johnny. We all love you so much. Just keep hanging in. Joel's on his way. And, John, don't worry about him. We'll take care of him for you. I promise you this." He found a patch of scalp that for some reason was still intact and kissed her there, then turned and left.

Whirling. That's how it felt. Everything was whirling around him. He had difficulty walking straight as he headed through the wing towards Labour and Delivery. He stopped and spoke with the nurse at the desk.

"Dr. Dante,I didn't expect to see you tonight. I don't think we have any or your patients in." The nurse noticed that his eyes were red and swollen, and he was unfocussed. "Are you alright, Dr.?"

"No, Didi. Where's Dr. Hopkins?"

"He's finishing up in room three. A healthy baby boy. He should be done in about five minutes."

Dominic tried to control the tremble that threatened to knock him off his feet. "Great. Listen, Didi, finish for him. I can't spare him that five minutes. I need him in the ER, stat. And after that, don't call on him for the rest of the night. If anything comes up call in somebody else." Instructions delivered, he turned and walked away before she could ask questions he didn't want to answer.

Joel walked into the lounge minutes later, concerned by the messsage. It was obvious that whatever the problem was, Dominic was distraught by it.

"What's wrong, Dom? They said it was an emergency."

"We don't have much time. There was a fire tonight. Someone got caught in the blaze and is severely burned. There's no chance of survival. I've seen the patient. I'm afraid I have to concur with Matt's prognosis."

"It must be someone close, or you wouldn't have called us all here," Joel said. "Who is it?"

Dominic took hold of Joel's hand, and with tears in his eyes, dropped the rings into it. "This is how they identified the body. I'm sorry, Joel."

Joel looked at the rings. Of course he recognized them. He'd bought them and looked at them every day for ten years, but how did Dominic get them? He didn't understand.

Joel looked at Dominic and whispered the dreaded word, "Johnica?"

Dominic nodded as he broke down and cried again, his hand clasped on Joel's knee. "I'm so sorry, Joel. You know we love Johnny."

"No, it's not Johnica. It's not. She's at night school tonight. She goes every Wednesday night. If we call the school we'll find she's there. She's teaching a literacy class. It's not Johnica." Denial would make it not true. If he kept denying it, it would all go away. It had to go away, because for Joel, there was no life without Johnny. She was a half of his whole.

"She's in the trauma room. We'll come in with you, but you don't have much time left. You don't have to do this alone." Having already seen what little was left of her, Dominic didn't want Joel to be on his own.

"The kids. What about the kids, Dom? Did anybody check on my children? Was the fire at my house? I want to know about my children."

Dominic looked at the floor and shook his head. "The children are fine, Joel. The fire wasn't at the house." He'd spoken to Tara Shepherd while waiting for his friends to arrive. Once again rising to his feet, he felt the weight of the world crushing down on his shoulders. "You'd better get in there to see her now.".

"Yeah, of course. She's still alive, right? If it's really her, she'll be fine. John won't leave me. She'll never leave me."

Dominic walked with him to the trauma room. Joel moved to the table and looked. If this was October, he'd believe they were playing a Halloween prank on him, but it was only February.

"Meghan, was there any other jewellery?"

"Yes, Dr. Hopkins. She had this necklace around her neck." She held out the blue topaz necklace he'd given Johnica for Valentine's Day two weeks ago and handed it to him, then along with the rest of the ER team, left them alone to say goodbye.

Joel looked at the necklace and felt his legs start to shake. "Oh, God! Oh, God!"

Leaning over the table he spoke. "Johnica? Honey, is it really you?" It was a stupid question and he knew it. Of course it was her. The way his heart was throbbing, he knew it was. "John, don't leave me, honey. Don't you remember this afternoon? We were so happy. Things are gonna change now, remember? I love you, darling. So much. You have to wake up so we can go home. Becca's gonna want feeding. She's probably hollering up a storm right now. Come on, John, you've always been there when she's needed you. You've always been there when any of us needed you. We can't be a family if you don't wake up and come home."

What small bit remained of the eyelids opened, and he could see her looking at him. He knew those blue eyes. He saw the single tear that trickled from one. "I love you, Johnica. I love you. I'll never stop." His voice broke and tears trickled down his cheeks.

148

She struggled to be able to say something to him, but the respirator made it impossible. To remove it would be instant death.

"Honey, don't leave me here. We all need you too much."

He fell to his knees, sobbing inconsolably when the monitor screamed that her heart was no longer beating.

Dominic stood at the foot of the table and quietly noted, "Time of death, 22:14." He reached over, switched off the monitors, and left Joel to privately grieve for his beautiful young wife that he had worshipped with his heart, with his hands, with his body. The one he would never be able to hold again, laugh with again, share secrets with again. The one who was here a moment ago and wasn't now. Her heart had stopped beating and so did his.

THE MOURNING SONG

Where is everything?
Where is that I know?
Covered tracks walked in snow.

Now I fall down
The hardest part is getting up I know
But as much as I strive
There is no spark
No coming alive
Nothing blooms within me
Nothing dares thrive.

There are steps that I've taken
All of them mistaken
Past the realm of the forsaken
Into the arms of sin
Past the ones that I love
Without a flinch or cringe.

How strange that you are there all along
Watching, singing a mourning song
Of what within me is laying still
That does not live nor ever will
Your cries bitter
Your song shrill

Kechelle Barness

AUTHOR BIOS

Andrea Allison has been published at Runesmag.com, Stories of Strength Anthology and Long Story Short. You can view her website at http://andreaallison.bravehost.com.

Dora Archer lives in Greece with her family and variety of animals. She attended the College of Charleston where she studied anthropology and has taken further coursework in writing and editing. Currently she is a technical consultant for a communications company and makes classic leather-bound journals on commission. She is a member of Writers Pen, an online authors help and critique group and in her free time she enjoys reading, photography and archery.

Kechelle Barness is twenty-two years. She was born and raised in the small town of Manjimup in Western Australia and currently resides there. She has been published in the online enzine Runes Mag.

Cynthia Bateman lives with her husband of nearly 30 years in the tiny town of Sumas, WA, snuggled up next to the Canada border. She considers herself a poet and has had several pieces published both online and in print as well as authoring an epic poem which has been published as a print book and an audio book. She also writes the occasional short story, dabbles in water colors and teaches art and writing to children. Her very most favorite pastime, however, is being a grandma. That's the best!

Carrie Chesney is the owner of Authors by Design. She is the author of The Lander Series: Christopher which was published by Archebooks in 2005, and TLS:Brody which was published by Westmorland Publishing in 2008. The next volume, Jennifer, is due out in the early spring of 2009. She has also co-authored The Secrets of Blaney's Mountain which is due out on bookshelves in November 2008. The above short story is an excerpt of TLS: Joel which you can look for in October 2009. Carrie lives with her husband, Lance, in Wisconsin. They are the parents of twelve children.

Jeannine Dufresne - During my second year in high school, the class project was to write a novel (any genre). It was a great experience and it developed my interest in writing. I share my life with my best friend Richard, and my tabby cat Charlie.

Virginia Lee Fair, born in Oklahoma, lived in California and upon retiring relocated to beautiful Cedar Bluff, Alabama. Writing since the age of ten, she progressed from poetry to fantasy writing. She worked for a number of years as the editor for the Head Start Academy newspaper in Rancho Cordova, California.
While currently working on a compilation of memoirs, she is in the process of writing a romance novel.

Susie Hawes - Susie's husband and children are patient, her housework is neglected and her dog is not speaking to her. Her work has appeared in Neo-Opsis, Andromeda Spaceways, Quietus, Surreal Magazine, and "The Shadowbox Anthology". "Necromancer's Curse" and "Necromancer's Redemption" were in the Fictionwise Dark Fantasy Best Sellers list. "The Dragon Creed", "Dragon Insurrection and "Dragon at Law" are available at fictionwise.com.

E.J. Hayes lives in Sydney where she spent time as a law student, air force officer, fundraiser, editorial assistant and musician before settling on writing as a career. She loves to write sexy tales about wild, wonderful and wicked fantasy creatures. Visit her website at www.ericahayes.net

Sharon Kasenberg has been prolifically penning poetry for the past few years. She has plans to make a compilation for publication in the near future. Sharon lives in Kitchener, Ontario with her husband and two boys.

Robin Layne lives in Oregon. She is managing editor of "Sweet Comfort," monthly newsletter of a mental health organization. She publishes poems and articles in the newsletter, and has published her poetry, nonfiction, and fiction elsewhere.

Jia Lin has been published in several online literary magazines, such as Verbsap, Storyglossia, Pequin and Blood Orange Review. She is currently a student at a small liberal college with plans to major in political science and minor in english.

Thomas Lynn born in St. Louis during the Great Depression and was a soldier and federal agent before retiring to Lawrenceville, Georgia. An award-winning poet, author and columnist, his fiction and poetry credits have appeared in various publications and anthologies. The mystery novel that he co-authored with Carrie Chesney, The Secrets of Blaney's Mountain, is due out in stores in the fall of 2008.

Tommie Lyn - What she learned while doing genealogical research spurred Tommie Lyn's desire to write. Since then, she has written two novels and several stories in different genres, from historical to mystery. She says, "Everyone has at least one story to tell. I've decided to write my stories down and share them."

Mike Massey has recently moved back home to Utah after a 21 year absence. He is active in community theater, working in all phases from acting to building sets and everything in between. He has been writing and telling stories in some form or another since he was old enough to hold a pencil. This will be his first published work.

Randi-Lee Ryder resides in Calgary, Alberta. Her poetry has been published in Oestara Publishing's 2006 Eppie Award winning poetry book "Anthology of Pagan Poetry." She has had short stories published in Runes E-zine and has previously written for a newspaper.

Carol Scarr writes short fiction in the speculative, mainstream, and dark fiction genres. She finds fault with software for a living, working as a software QA engineer in southern Ohio. She lives with her British husband and loves to travel but hates to pack